"*I u a client very well.*"

"Sage, it wasn't like that! You said yourself, courting clients is standard practice."

"Yes, courting them openly at dinner, when both parties know exactly what's going on. It isn't standard practice to let on you care for someone when you're only trying to put a fast one over on her. That's despicable."

"Sage, it wasn't like that! I wanted to tell you this— to confess about last weekend. I've been wanting to tell you everything from the start."

"What was stopping you?"

"I assumed that you'd—you would reach the very conclusion you've just reached. That I was only after your property."

"Afraid I'd wake up and smell the stench of your sort of business dealings, you mean."

"I'm sorry. Can't we go somewhere and talk about this? Have lunch?"

"I'm a little particular about who I have lunch with. Go find yourself another dupe, Mr. Jameson."

Dear Reader,

It's May—spring gardens are in full bloom, and in the spirit of the season, we've gathered a special "bouquet" of Silhouette Romance novels for you this month.

Whatever the season, Silhouette Romance novels *always* capture the magic of love with compelling stories that will make you laugh and cry; stories that will move you with the wonder of romance, time and again.

This month, we continue our FABULOUS FATHERS series with Melodie Adams's heartwarming novel, *What About Charlie?* Clint Blackwell might be the local hero when it comes to handling troubled boys, but he never met a rascal like six-year-old Charlie Whitney. And he never met a woman like Charlie's lovely mother, Candace, who stirs up trouble of a different kind in the rugged cowboy's heart.

With drama and emotion, Moyra Tarling takes us to the darker side of love in *Just a Memory Away.* After a serious accident, Alison Montgomery is unable to remember her past. She struggles to learn the truth about her handsome husband, Nick, and a secret about their marriage that might be better left forgotten.

There's a passionate battle of wills brewing in Joleen Daniels's *Inheritance.* The way Jude Emory sees it, beautiful Margret Brolin has stolen the land and inheritance that is rightfully his. How could a man as proud as Jude let her steal his heart as well?

Please join us in welcoming new author Lauryn Chandler who debuts this month with a lighthearted love story, *Mr. Wright.* We're also proud to present *Can't Buy Me Love* by Joan Smith and *Wrangler* by Dorsey Kelley.

In the months to come, watch for books by more of your favorites—Diana Palmer, Suzanne Carey, Elizabeth August, Marie Ferrarella and many more. At Silhouette, we're dedicated to bringing you the love stories you love to read. Our authors and editors want to hear from you. Please write to us; we take our reader comments to heart.

Happy reading!

Anne Canadeo
Senior Editor

CAN'T BUY ME LOVE
Joan Smith

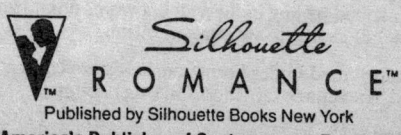

Published by Silhouette Books New York
America's Publisher of Contemporary Romance

If you purchased this book without a cover you should be aware that this book is stolen property. It was reported as "unsold and destroyed" to the publisher, and neither the author nor the publisher has received any payment for this "stripped book."

 SILHOUETTE BOOKS
300 East 42nd St., New York, N.Y. 10017

CAN'T BUY ME LOVE

Copyright © 1993 by Joan Smith

All rights reserved. Except for use in any review, the reproduction or utilization of this work in whole or in part in any form by any electronic, mechanical or other means, now known or hereafter invented, including xerography, photocopying and recording, or in any information storage or retrieval system, is forbidden without the permission of the publisher, Silhouette Books, 300 E. 42nd St., New York, N.Y. 10017

ISBN: 0-373-08935-X

First Silhouette Books printing May 1993

All the characters in this book have no existence outside the imagination of the author and have no relation whatsoever to anyone bearing the same name or names. They are not even distantly inspired by any individual known or unknown to the author, and all incidents are pure invention.

®: Trademark used under license and registered in the United States Patent and Trademark Office and in other countries.

Printed in the U.S.A.

Books by Joan Smith

Silhouette Romance

Next Year's Blonde #234
Caprice #255
From Now On #269
Chance of a Lifetime #288
Best of Enemies #302
Trouble in Paradise #315
Future Perfect #325
Tender Takeover #343
The Yielding Art #354
The Infamous Madam X #430
Where There's a Will #452
Dear Corrie #546
If You Love Me #562
By Hook or By Crook #591
After the Storm #617
Maybe Next Time #635
It Takes Two #656
Thrill of the Chase #669
Sealed with a Kiss #711
Her Nest Egg #755
Her Lucky Break #795
For Richer, for Poorer #838
Getting To Know You #879
Headed for Trouble #919
Can't Buy Me Love #935

JOAN SMITH

has written many Regency romances, but likes working with the greater freedom of contemporaries. She also enjoys mysteries and Gothics, collects Japanese porcelain and is a passionate gardener. A native of Canada, she is the mother of three. This is her twenty-fifth Silhouette Romance novel!

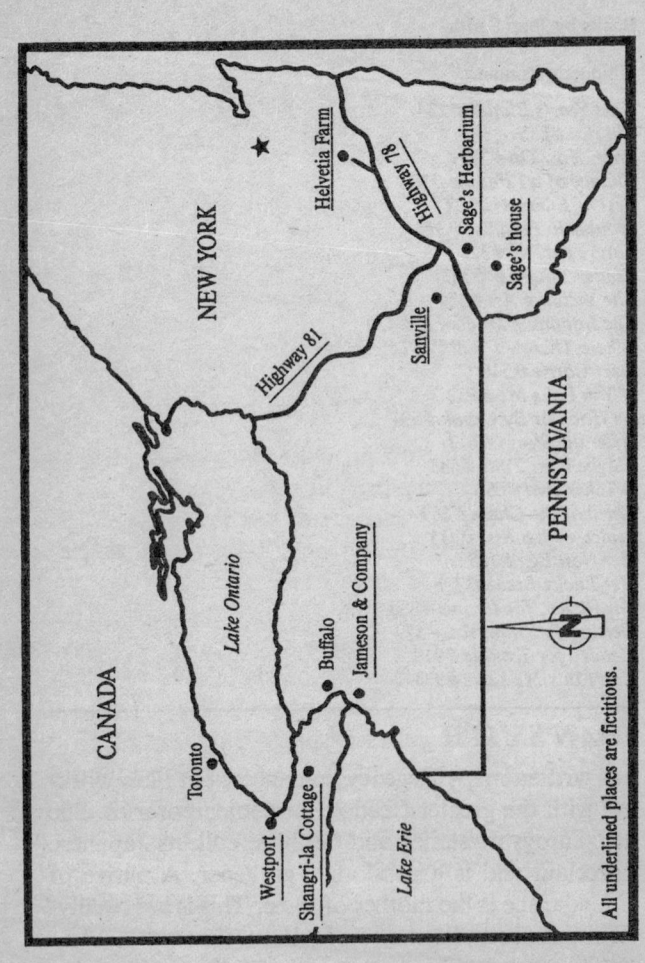

Chapter One

Sage Cramer shut off her word processor, leaned back and began massaging her stiff neck. The digital clock on her desk pulsed the seconds as the hour changed from three fifty-nine to four o'clock. That was enough writing for one day. She had her article for next week's column on herbs composed in rough, to be polished later. She smiled at the title, "Sage Advice."

Her writing on herbs had begun as a hobby. Next it had grown into a brochure for her herb shop. The editor-in-chief of the local newspaper had seen it and asked her to do a weekly column. Soon after, a small newspaper chain had discovered her work, which was picked up for syndication in their ten weeklies. The manager of the chain had told her a few larger dailies had expressed interest. Nothing had come of it yet, but the future looked bright. She had just begun to toy with the idea of consolidating her columns into a book. Some hobby!

Sage felt a thrill of satisfaction as she ticked off item number four on her list: write article for paper. Making lists was indicative of compulsive behavior, which was a part of her mental makeup. Scooping up the litter of research papers on the extension arm of her desk, Sage returned them to the folder marked Chamomile. This craving for tidiness was also symptomatic of her tendencies.

It was a carry-over from her days with the consulting firm Baxter and Associates. If you didn't have your work organized there, you were lost. A day seldom passed that she didn't thank her lucky stars for her decision to leave that rat race. Up at seven, gulp a cup of coffee, dash to the station, commute downtown, attend meetings, work the phone to calm and cajole clients, prepare reports, and grab a sandwich at your desk, if you didn't have a business lunch. Sage had usually worked a twelve-hour day, as she'd often taken her job home with her. And for what? Was the world really a better place because she closed a profitable deal for Mike Baxter?

She'd had enough of that. When her old boss, Mike Baxter, had retired, his son took over. Young Mike's way of running the business was very different from his father's. Within a month, Sage knew she couldn't be happy working for the young upstart. It wasn't his slave-driving management style that repelled her so much as his sleazy business practices. He'd do anything for a buck. He had temporarily increased the firm's revenue, but at the cost of its good reputation.

It was Grandpa Cramer's death that finally catapulted her into resigning. He had left his farm in upstate New York to her. As with most small dairy farms, it was a precarious financial operation. Her neighbor to the north had given up on farming and moved to the city. McGregor's farm was just boarded up, awaiting a sale that never seemed to come. If it was still available in a couple of years when she was better off financially, Sage hoped to buy the property and set up a riding stable. John Newton, the neighbor to the south, made no secret that he'd sell if he could make enough to retire. Someone had taken an option on his farm, but Sage doubted anything would come of it.

Her grandpa's farm was still working, but not as a dairy farm. Sage grew herbs commercially. She had used her marketing and management skills to turn the farm into a going concern—and she continued to work twelve-hour days. The difference was that she did it on her own time and terms, and loved every minute of it.

It was only this room, her office, that gave any clue to her past employment. She had set about establishing her herb farm and outlets, both wholesale and retail, as efficiently and professionally as possible. All her customer records and accounting were on computer. A row of green filing cabinets flanked one wall. The other wall was filled by a pair of desks, each fronted by a wheeled office chair.

The severity of office furniture and slatted blinds was softened by the framed prints of herbs. Their green foliage was a background to the delicate indigo tints of chicory, lavender and hyssop, the golden yellow of curry and dill, the pink of comfrey and valerian. Hanging pots of ivy and fern formed a lacy curtain at the window.

With a last, loving look at her office, she switched off the light and went upstairs to change into her bathing suit. The remainder of the house was much as her grandparents had left it. Her grandfather hadn't changed a thing when his wife died three years ago. The furnishings were elderly objects, not fine antiques. The decorative touches were simple milk glass and brass candlesticks, not crystal and silver.

The matched walnut bedroom suite in her bedroom had come from a catalog, but in the days when they made things of real wood and even added a little carving. Her grandmother had crocheted the brightly colored afghan covering her bed. It was the old-fashioned kind with multicolored squares held together by black wool. It added a splash of color to the pastel walls, and the pale green carpet Sage had bought to replace an ancient rug.

Various hues of green ran like a theme throughout the interior of the house, which always seemed to be such a comforting color to Sage. It took her back to her days in the commune her parents had belonged to when she was a child. Her memories of those years were vague but happy. The family had left the year Sage entered school. Despite the large number of adults around, the children had been given a great deal of freedom. She remembered playing in meadows spangled with buttercups and daisies, much like the fields surrounding this farm.

Then suddenly the flower power era of the sixties was over. Her parents had gotten divorced, and she'd lived with her mother in a series of rented apartments, each smaller and dingier than the one before. She remembered her mother complaining about the shortage of money. "We can't afford it, Sage," was often heard. She had no bicycle like the other kids, no pretty clothes, no money for movies or toys.

These extremely difficult times were responsible for her vow to never be poor again. When her mother remarried, she had left Sage behind with her paternal grandparents, to avoid interrupting her schooling. Sage was fifteen then, old enough to speak for herself. She didn't get along with her new stepfather, and the grandparents had not only offered, but begged to take her.

After high school, Sage had studied business, serving tables and working during the summer to help pay her tuition, and when she graduated, she'd joined the rat race with a vengeance. Fast track all the way, until she was burned out in three years.

But all that was behind her now. Her father, she'd heard, had moved to Canada. Her mother's second marriage hadn't lasted long. The third husband seemed to be working out better. Sage wrote to her mom and they talked on the phone every week, but the only daily reminder of her past was her name, Sage. Her mother had told her an old Arab proverb. "How can a man die who has sage in his garden?" she had said.

"Will you live forever, Mom?" a worried Sage had asked.

"A part of me will, through you and your children."

Sage wanted to have children, but not just yet. Not until she could be sure they would have all the things she had done without. And more important than having money was finding the right husband and father. He must be a man who would always be there, for them and for her.

There was sage growing in the garden at the farm, planted in a sunny, well-drained corner where it thrived, as all her plants did. Location and soil, those were the requirements. In a fanciful mood, Sage thought it applied to people, too, in a way. Their "soil" was the job that nourished them, their sunlight was a sound, loving family. She had not thrived at Baxter and Associates after Mike, senior, had retired, but she flourished here, at the farm, with her Aunt May Cramer.

Sage changed into a simple black one-piece bathing suit, picked up her towel and ran downstairs, out the back door to the pool her grandpa had built especially for her. Her employees used it now, too. As they were still busy at four o'clock, however, she had it to herself. Stopping a moment, she looked admiringly at the little sparkling kidney-shaped pool, set amid a bower of tumbling flowers: simple annuals, petunias and lobelias, impatiens and begonias.

One day she would have a proper English garden of perennials. There was plenty of space for one. Space seemed a luxury to her after having lived in a city apartment.

Sage dived in and let the water and exercise wash away her cramps—mental and physical. When she was totally relaxed, she toweled her long honey-blond hair and ran a comb through it, drying it in the sun. She was suddenly eager to visit her herb shop, and couldn't wait to go upstairs and dress. She'd just slip into the flowered mumu her mom had sent her from Hawaii. She stepped into her thongs, snatched the flowing robe from the back door of the kitchen, and went around to the shop.

She had painted Grandpa Cramer's old livery stable wedgwood blue, added cream shutters and a Dutch door, and found an old weathercock in an antique store to decorate the roof. A bell jangled when she opened the door and stepped inside. The delicious scent of potpourri perfumed the air. Sunlight filtered in at the windows, glinting off glass jars and the old-fashioned, ornate cash register, which was a work of art.

It was like walking into the past. Her salesclerks wore long dresses and mobcaps. Along the counter ranged the sparkling bottles of dried herbs. More dried herbs hung in bundles from the ceiling, and fresh ones were kept fresh in water. Other goods were displayed on shelves and in bins. She took in her neighbors' homey wares on consignment, as well. Scented candles, dried flower arrangements, homemade jams and jellies, breads and cakes, and some hand-thrown pottery.

As the salesclerks were busy, Sage didn't interrupt them. She made a surreptitious head count: nine customers. Not bad, when you took into account that most customers had to drive out from the city. Her eyes moved toward the corner where baked goods were sold. Marjorie Allan's carrot muffins smelled too good to resist, which prompted her to take one. She fished a coin out of her pocket to pay for it and left it on the counter. The clerk smiled, acknowledging the gesture made by her employer.

Sage left, nibbling the muffin, to stroll through the Elizabethan knot garden. She had planted a decorative herb knot garden in front of the shop to set the mood. The heady aroma of low-growing herbs was released as her ankles brushed the foliage. Absorbed in thought, she didn't notice the man getting out of the sports car that had just driven into the parking lot. She wouldn't have paid much attention if she had. Dark glasses concealed that he was staring at her with an assessing gleam in his eyes.

In the office of Jameson and Company, Wilf Jameson took a deep breath to keep from exploding. Why had he ever gone into business with his cousin, Ken Carson?

"I *know* we have an option on Newton's farm, Ken," he said. "What you were *supposed* to be doing upstate was to get one on the Cramer place."

Ken Carson scratched his wrinkled brow in confusion. Although he was only thirty, the hair was already receding in half moons from his forehead, which added an illusion of length to his chubby face. Nothing about his features or personality could give any illusion of intelligence. He lived in a constant state of confusion. When his father had died and left him a great deal of money, he'd turned to Cousin Wilf as to a savior, to help him manage it. Wilf had a nose for business. With Wilf as a partner, Ken's fortune had doubled in five years.

"You said we need about two hundred acres. McGregor's is a hundred. Newton's is over a hundred. That's more than two hundred acres."

"Yes, but a golf course needs the two hundred acres to be all in one piece, not with a hundred and fifty acres coming between them. That's a long trek between holes. There's no point in our buying up two farms if we don't own the one in the middle," Wilf explained patiently.

"Maybe we could do something else with the two properties. You mentioned a health spa. And there's tennis..."

Wilf Jameson's dark blue eyes frowned in impatience. "My study indicates that area is starving for another golf course. The established courses have a backlog of golfers waiting to get in. Cramer's farm has the perfect terrain. Some nice hills, terrific scenery, and gravel scattered about the property made to order for sand pits. We wouldn't even have to import sand for the traps. The only problem is that it isn't quite large enough. We need Newton's place, as well, which is why I took out the option on it."

"The thing is," Ken said apologetically, "the Cramer place is a going concern, Wilf. You won't pick it up for an old song. It has its own store and everything."

"I know the woman who inherited it opened a little store after she sold off the cattle. That tells me she isn't making a living on the farm itself. If she's smart, she'll snatch at an offer. It would be good business for her. I hope she isn't one of those die-hard farmers who think all real estate developers are evil."

"She was very pretty," Ken said, with a dreamy look in his blue eyes. Wilf gave him a derisive look. "The store seemed to be doing a pretty good business," he said in a more businesslike way. "I bought some herbal tea. It's like a tranquilizer. Put me right to sleep, and you know how much trouble I have sleeping when I'm on the road."

"Herbal tea," Wilf said dismissively. "She certainly isn't making any fortune on that. If she sells, she could open up shop in a shopping mall, and draw ten times as many customers. Point out to her—"

Wilf came to a stop. Ken was a good man to deal with country customers. His open face and forthright manner inspired trust. What Wilf Jameson was doing wasn't dishonest or even sleazy, but as soon as a farmer heard the word "developer," he turned suspicious.

Optimizing land use was just common sense. He didn't cheat his customers, but he knew that real estate developers had a bad reputation. And there was something in him that denoted the air of big business. Maybe it was his looks, or his clothes, or his car, but Wilf wasn't about to change himself just to bring a deal to fruition.

On the other hand, if the pretty woman who owned Cramer's place was any sort of businesswoman, she'd make mincemeat of Ken. She might demand—and get—an inordinate price for her hundred and fifty acres of not very fertile farmland. He'd better see her himself.

He'd drive up to Cramer's place and see just what he was up against. The drive north from Buffalo was through pretty countryside. The area was booming, but as he got farther north, the traffic thinned. This country club he had in mind would be a showplace, drawing clientele from half a dozen small communities. A great tourist spot in the summer, too, with Niagara Falls within commuting distance. The layout of the land, viewed from a helicopter, told him it had the potential to become a first-rate golf course. If they could draw some of the big tournaments in, his and Ken's country club would soon be known nationally.

Wilf came to attention when he entered a small town called Sanville. Cramer's place was on a side route just five miles north of it. He was relieved to see that he would be traveling on a paved road. Subjecting his low-slung sports car to a natural dirt path would be the equivalent of cruelty to animals or child abuse. A pointing finger sign informed him the Herbarium was just three miles farther along. As he passed Newton's place, he imagined the clubhouse sitting on that rise of land where a rundown white clapboard farmhouse now sat. It gave a commanding view of the countryside.

A few minutes later he saw a quaint red brick farmhouse, and the Herbarium sign posted modestly beside the mailbox. Sage Cramer, Prop. Funny name, Sage. Forgetful of Ken's description, the image of a delicately proportioned spinster with gray hair pinched back in a bun formed in his mind. As he parked his car and got out, he noticed a young woman walking through a little garden. She looked like a flower child of the sixties' hippie movement in a long dress and sandals, her blond hair streaming down her back.

Wilf was about to walk past her into the shop when she looked up. He noticed she was eating something. He continued into the shop and looked around. The place had plenty of customers, but how profitable could it be, selling candles and cookies, with about a hundred and forty-eight of the hundred and fifty acres just sitting idle? The clerks' long dresses and mobcaps struck him as a corny effort to establish a homespun country atmosphere. He asked for Miss Sage Cramer, and was directed out to the knot garden.

So Sage Cramer was the flower child munching on a muffin! Hesitating at first, he quickly devised the best approach. The first rule of thumb for any negotiation always began with a compliment, to establish friendly relations. He'd play it by ear, and make a tentative offer just before leaving. He'd let her mull it over. People didn't like to be rushed; they felt you were trying to put something over on them.

Wilf opened the door, then strode over to the knot garden. Sage was just picking a sprig of thyme and tasting it. "Miss Cramer?" Wilf beckoned to her in a friendly voice. At close range, he saw that her eyes were a dreamy sea green outlined with a sweep of black lashes. Her skin was innocent of cosmetics, not even lipstick, but she wasn't lacking in natural color. A breeze lifted her long hair away from her shoulders, tossing it about her face. She brushed it back with a practiced gesture.

Sage looked up, startled that this stranger knew her name. Her first thought was that he was an acquaintance from her business days. Everything about him suggested business. He wore his crisp black hair short and neatly barbered. His authoritative voice didn't have the ring of the country. The blue Oxford shirt hugging his broad shoulders was decorated with a tie, and his fawn trousers doubtlessly had a matching jacket in that fancy car he'd driven up in. Maybe it was the dark glasses that kept her from recognizing him.

"Do I know you?" she asked.

His hand shot out and gripped hers in a firm shake as his lips formed into what Sage considered a business smile, which was devoid of any genuine warmth. The sprig of thyme fell to the ground. "Wilfred Jameson," he said.

She conjured with the name, trying to place it. It definitely didn't ring any bells. "From Buffalo?" she asked.

"That's right. This is a lovely place you have here."

"Thank you."

"Homey—the shop."

"Yes. What is it you want, Mr. Jameson?"

"A little of your time, if you can spare it."

"Thyme?" she asked, in confusion. "The herbs are sold in the shop."

Wilf was temporarily at a loss. Just what was in that muffin the woman had been eating? "About five minutes, if you can spare it," he said in some confusion.

She glanced at her wrist, but she had removed her watch for swimming. Now where had she put it? Had she left it at the pool?

As Wilf watched her, he began to entertain some doubts as to her intelligence. She was as pretty as Ken had said, but it was an otherworldly sort of beauty. Her long hair blew in the wind, giving her the air of a wood nymph. Her large green eyes had a vague, questioning look. He thought of Shakespeare's beautiful but mad Ophelia. Maybe it was meeting her in a garden that brought that to mind.

"I guess I can spare five minutes," she said, and led him through a vine-covered pergola leading to the farmhouse. Patches of sunlight dappled the flagstone walk. A wicker table and chairs occupied the veranda. She sat down and indicated the other chair.

Wilf was happy to get out of the sun and when he drew off his dark glasses, Sage found herself being examined by a pair of intensely intelligent, dark blue eyes. His half-handsome, half-craggy features were accentuated by a strong jaw and ingratiating smile. She waited for him to speak, as she had no idea what this businessman could possibly want with her.

"This is a lovely place," he repeated.

"You already said that, Mr. Jameson."

"You live here alone, Miss Cramer?"

"No, I don't," she replied. What business was it of his?

"I was just thinking, it must be lonely for you."

So that was it! Another man trying to buy the farm. They always took the same approach, first complimenting her, then pointing out what they imagined to be the disadvantages of a woman running a farm. Any incipient interest she had been feeling in Mr. Jameson evaporated. She'd be polite, but she'd get rid of him quickly. "Lonely, with all those people in the shop?" she asked.

"It's an interesting little shop."

"I like it."

Seeing that this conversation was going nowhere, Wilf decided to take the plunge. "It's not very good use of a hundred and fifty acres though, is it?"

"I grow herbs," she said. Oh yes, he was definitely a developer.

Wilf noticed her lack of interest in his inquiry. The green eyes staring back at him were glazed with a mixture of boredom and annoyance. "On all the land?" he asked, knowing that ninety-nine percent of it was unused.

"Not yet, but I'm expanding. If you've come to make an offer on the farm, I might as well tell you it isn't for sale," she said.

His heart sank. Word of his plans had been leaked, and she was going to demand the moon and stars. He was disappointed, but by no means despondent. "You haven't heard my offer yet," he said, trying for a cheerful tone.

"You must be the man who took an option on Newton's farm," she said, not angrily, nor even very interested. She waited, but he didn't deny or confirm it. "If your plans for development depend on my farm, I'm afraid you've lost your option money. My farm isn't for sale."

Wilf had heard that before. It was usually a precursor to some hard bargaining, because in his experience, every property had its price. "As I said, you haven't heard my offer," he said temptingly.

"Let me hear it then," she said in a pleasantly polite voice that suggested she was humoring a lunatic.

Wilf did some swift calculations and named a price ten thousand dollars higher than he had intended offering. She didn't quite laugh in his face, but she continued smiling.

"Now I've heard your offer, and I'm still not interested," she said.

"It's more than the place is worth!" he objected.

"Not to me. Money isn't everything."

Damn! She knew he needed this farm, so he'd have to go higher. "It isn't necessarily my final offer," he said.

"Then why don't you quit wasting our time, and get to the bottom line?"

He studied her a moment. She was a strange woman. That dreamy look was back on her face. It was going to be hard to do business with a woman who didn't appreciate the value of money. Yet he doubted that Ophelia would speak of "the bottom line" in that practiced way.

"I never rush a seller. I don't like to be rushed myself," he said, to gain time to think.

"We're different in that respect. I don't like to waste time. I'd be wasting yours if I left you with the idea that the farm's for sale, at any price. You can't put a price on dreams, Mr. Jameson."

If this was some sixties' "flower power" philosophy, he wasn't interested. If, as was also possible, it was an attempt to up his price, he wasn't going to pay hard cash for her dreams. "Did we both dream that little shop?" he asked. "If your dream is to run a boutique in the style of the nineteenth century, you'd draw more customers in the city. Statistics show that more people shop in malls than—"

"Statistics sometimes lie," she pointed out. "And anyway, I couldn't grow my herbs in a mall."

"You could buy them wholesale. It'd probably be cheaper in the long run."

"Buy them!" she scoffed, showing the first signs of animation. "I sell fresh produce, organically grown to protect the environment. The fun is in growing them, not selling them."

Oh Lord, a health nut! He might have known. "I wouldn't think upstate New York is the ideal location for growing herbs. A pretty short growing season. If you moved south, you could get a couple of crops a year."

"I take it, from what you're saying, that you don't plan to use these local farms for growing anything, except maybe high-rise apartment houses," she said. Her eyes accused him.

It was a constant aggravation to Wilf that people took this high moral tone about developing high-rise apartments or condominiums. "Not everyone is fortunate enough to be able to afford a home. What are the others supposed to do, live on the street?" he retorted.

"I have nothing against apartment buildings. I just don't see why you people have to build them in the country, paving over good farmland."

"This farmland is not particularly good, but in fact I wasn't planning to develop it for housing."

"What, then?"

A developer never revealed his intention until he had his deal sewed up. If the competition got wind of it, he might find himself outbid. "I'm not at liberty to say," he said.

"Well, I am at liberty to say categorically that my farm isn't on the market."

"But you can't possibly be making any money on this," he said, flinging his hand vaguely toward the shop.

She leaned forward, her chin resting on her knuckles. Mr. Jameson looked tense and unhappy. He looked frustrated, and hot and tired. He looked like a man who was rapidly working himself into an early grave. She could sympathize with that. She took pity on him, and when she spoke, she spoke gently.

"There's more to life than making money, Mr. Jameson. I know it's a cliché, but like most clichés, it's true. You should take some time off to relax. You should get a hobby. Play golf, or tennis, or something."

Golf! How did she come to mention that? "I love my work!"

"You mean you actually enjoy badgering people?"

"I'm not badgering you. This is a unique business opportunity—"

"I've had three of these 'unique' business opportunities since I inherited the farm. I told the others what I'm telling you. Not interested. Sorry. Was there anything else?" she asked in an effort to be rid of him.

Wilf drew a deep sigh. It was five o'clock. He didn't relish the long drive back to Buffalo. And since the option on Newton's farm was running out, he wanted another chance to "badger" Miss Cramer. He wondered if she might be less hostile over dinner.

"Maybe you could recommend a hotel nearby," he said.

"The Belview in Sanville is pretty good. They have a pool and, of course, TV."

"I guess it'll be a solitary dinner and TV then," he said, peering to see if she pitied his lonesome, boring itinerary for the night.

"I recommend the ribs—if you like ribs." Her green eyes laughed at his blatant bid for sympathy.

"Do you like ribs?"

"Yes, but I believe I smelled a chicken roasting as I went through the kitchen. My aunt does the cooking. I don't live alone," she said. She and May didn't plan to eat that chicken tonight either, but she didn't have to tell him that. "You asked, before, when you were trying to make me realize that I was isolated here, and would be better off in a hot, bustling city."

"I guess I wasn't as subtle as I thought I was," he said with an apologetic smile.

Mr. Jameson looked much more attractive when his rugged features relaxed into a smile. Sage had admired his looks and broad shoulders as soon as she had seen him. She sometimes missed the companionship of the professional people she used to work with. In a way, she admired their hard-driving energy and ambition. She loved her new life, too, but she didn't want to become a country mouse, cut off entirely from her past. It might be amusing to spend an evening with Mr. Jameson. Besides, she was curious to discover what he was up to.

"I can only give you a *C* for effort," she joked. "It lacked originality."

If it was originality the lady wanted, Wilf felt he could oblige. He pondered what might be novel for a woman living on a farm, and soon had an idea. That fellow he had hired to give him a helicopter ride over the area lived nearby. He was always eager to get a customer. The view should be pretty at night, with the lights from the surrounding towns sparkling below.

"That was because I kept both feet on the ground," he said. Sage sensed some ulterior meaning, and looked a question at him. "Tonight I mean to take to the air. Interested?"

"Are we talking about a flight to Paris, or a ride in Herman Hooten's helicopter?" she asked.

Wilf's smile stretched to a grin. "Whichever one you like. Actually it was Hooten's helicopter I had in mind. I take it you've already done that?"

"He gives rides at all the fairs."

"It's hard to be inventive when you don't know the territory intimately."

Sage made up her mind on the spot. She'd see Mr. Jameson that evening, but on her own terms. "This is my turf. I'll show you something highly inventive, Mr. Jameson."

"Wilf," he said, smiling.

"Wilf. I guess Aunt May's chicken will keep. I'll pick you up at the hotel at six-thirty."

"I'll be at the Belview at Sanville."

"Good. I'll call for you there."

"This is very kind of you, Sage. I appreciate it. You wouldn't care to give me a hint..."

"It's a surprise, but bring your appetite." She sparkled a coquettish smile at him.

When Wilf left, his hopes soaring, Sage scurried into the kitchen. May Cramer was just taking a chicken out of the oven. The younger sister of Sage's grandfather, she kept house for Sage. The former schoolteacher had taken an early retirement, after which she had blossomed into a free spirit, donning an outlandish mode of style and dress she had always craved but felt her profession prohibited.

She had bleached her rusty hair blond, wore a great deal of makeup, and chose the brightest clothes she could find. She'd had three offers of marriage in two years, but was waiting for Mr. Right. Meanwhile, she was learning how to cook and run a house.

"I'll let this cool off a little before I put it in the fridge," she said, looking doubtfully at a charred bird. "It'll make a nice chicken salad tomorrow. It's only the skin that's singed. On these hot days, a cold meal is nice."

"Great. I invited a man to the strawberry social with us tonight, May. I hope you don't mind?"

"Mind? I'm delighted. Who is he?"

"A man named Wilf Jameson. He's trying to buy the farm."

"Another one? How old?"

"Oh, thirtyish. Tall, dark and handsome."

"Too bad he's not fifty, but it's the style for older ladies to date younger men. Or is he yours?"

"Well, I think he plans to try to sweet talk me into selling the farm, but if you can rope him, he's yours."

May's soft giggles followed Sage up the stairs. She wondered what Mr. City Slicker would think when he saw they were to have a chaperon. That should be imaginative enough for Mr. Jameson.

Chapter Two

In the heat of summer, Sage usually wore her hair up to keep cool. She drew it loosely on top of her head, allowing a few tendrils to escape to soften the effect. She chose a flowered dress that nipped in at her small waist and ended at mid-calf in a whirl of ruffles. As she examined herself in her mirror, it occurred to her that her professional friends would scarcely recognize her, but this Western look would suit the strawberry social. Besides, it made her feel romantic.

It was clear to Sage that Wilf Jameson was only going out with her because he was interested in her farm. Even though his intentions were glaringly apparent, there was no reason why they couldn't become friends. Friendship had to begin somewhere. Besides which, she hadn't met many interesting men since she'd left her city job, at least not until Wilf made his presence known.

Unlike Sage, May Cramer had no thought of romance as she dressed for the evening. After one of her current beaux had told her that he would be unable to attend the social, May decided to dress casually, choosing to wear white culottes with a brilliant blue halter top that exposed her freckled shoulders. To shield her eyes from the setting sun, she added a straw hat with a vividly colored ribbon encircling the band and trailing down her back.

"It isn't a costume party, is it? We used to dress like that in the fifties," she said, with a squint at her niece's outfit when Sage came downstairs.

"Everything old is new again, May. And besides," Sage added with a mischievous grin, "I don't want to look too urban. I promised Mr. Jameson an original evening."

"I see. You're letting on you're a hayseed, in other words. We'd better take your van. Your Porsche would give the show away."

"I should get rid of my car, but it handles so well." Sage was reluctant to give up this symbol of her successful career. About the only time she drove it now was when she got dressed up to meet her old friends for lunch in the city, but she couldn't bear to part with it.

At six-thirty she parked the van in front of the Belview. Wilf Jameson was waiting for her in the lobby. Not knowing what to expect, he had dressed in a business suit, but carried his jacket over his shoulder. There was no mistaking him for anything but a successful businessman. He looked so handsome Sage was a little sorry she hadn't gone urban and worn something chic to impress him.

"Your chariot awaits, Wilf," she said, making a playful curtsy.

As he held the door and followed her out to the van, his eyes made a practiced sweep of her outfit. It appealed to the latent romantic in him. Those curls flirting around her ears were charming. So was the glimpse of thin ankles beneath that billowing skirt. He mentally spanned her small waist with his two hands. She was certainly a different type from the more voluptuously built women he usually went out with. He looked forward to this evening. At the van, he noticed there was someone in the back seat, and assumed Sage was dropping a friend off en route.

"This is my aunt, May Cramer. She's coming with us," Sage said, watching him from the corner of her eye. She suppressed a gurgle of laughter when his mouth dropped open.

But he quickly recovered. "How nice. I'm charmed to meet you, May." He got into the van, still wondering where they were going.

"I hope you brought your appetite," Sage said.

"I usually eat a little later, but I am hungry. It must be this good country air."

Sage drove onto the highway and joined the row of cars heading to St. Alban's churchyard. Wilf realized some local festivity was in progress, but assumed they would be going on to some special restaurant. He was surprised when Sage turned the van into the parking lot with the other traffic.

A banner was raised on two posts. Welcome To St. Alban's Annual Strawberry Social was scrawled by hand across it.

"This is certainly original," Wilf said softly when Sage turned off the ignition. His eyes just skimmed to the back seat, where May was scrabbling out of her seat belt. His look acknowledged that Sage had played a trick on him, and his glinting eyes even hinted at revenge.

"You'll love it," May said. "I made a casserole of scalloped potatoes myself. From scratch. I plan to avoid it. If you're wise, you'll do the same. It's a red bowl. You'll recognize it by the black on top. Darned oven isn't working right."

Wilf put a hand on one elbow of each of the women to traverse the uneven ground to the trestle tables covered with paper tablecloths. The crowd was in a holiday mood, laughing and talking. He seated the women first, then had the unenviable task of trying to reach his own seat between them. It was awkward getting his legs over the bench, but he managed it without jarring his companions.

"You have a choice of ham or ham, with scalloped potatoes and salad," May informed him. "I hope you like ham."

His "Yes, indeed" lacked conviction.

Hearty portions were served on paper plates to facilitate cleaning up afterward. The food was certainly good and plentiful, but it wasn't the sort of evening Wilf had been imagining. He favored candlelight, wine and soft music. And preferably a little privacy.

The table was so crowded that May kept poking him with her elbow. Three young boys seated across from them kept up a noisy barrage of laughter and loud talk. Wilf knew it was only a matter of time until one of them spilled his drink. There it went! A dark ooze of cola flowed toward his plate. He managed to catch most of the overflow with his paper serviette, but his trousers would have to go to the cleaners.

Sage smiled apologetically and put a few more paper serviettes over the wet table cover. "Kids," she said forgivingly. "Have you ever been to one of these events before, Wilf?"

"This is a first," he said through thin lips.

"And a last?" she asked with a teasing look.

Had she brought him here to discourage him? To teach him a lesson, maybe? "On the contrary. It's a nice change," he assured her.

"Now this is what I call a treat!" May exclaimed when a bowl of strawberry shortcake replaced the ham.

He had to agree with her on that. The coffee that followed was strong and freshly brewed, just the way he liked it. His thanks after were warmer than Sage had expected.

After dinner they strolled around the grounds, where various games of chance were in progress. May expressed an interest in playing bingo, but Sage thought this was a little too much to subject Wilf to, and begged off.

"You run along, then," May said. "I plan to win that pink teddy bear for my goddaughter. I'll hitch a ride home with the Newtons."

Sage and Wilf returned to the van. It was just eight o'clock, and in the long days of late June, the sky was still light. Tints of peach verged into petal pink, and faded into amethyst. Sage stood a moment, gazing at it. "Isn't that pretty? You don't see skies like that in the city."

"I believe city folks enjoy the same sky as country folks," he said.

"Yes, but they don't see it for the pollution."

"It's nice," Wilf said rather stiffly. He didn't know quite how to behave. At times, he got the idea Sage was teasing him, or maybe testing him. If she had arranged this outing to teach him some sort of lesson, he wanted to retaliate. On the other hand, he still needed her farm, and didn't intend to antagonize her needlessly.

"Sorry about your trousers," she said. "I thought you might enjoy the social more than eating alone."

She sounded sincere. "I did, certainly. Having a drink with you would be better than watching television too," he said, looking an invitation at her.

"I guess I could have one drink. There's a bar at the Belview."

A piano tinkled on a raised stage in the dim bar. If there were any decorative touches to the place, it was too dark to see them. A few customers were dancing. Taking a table in the far corner, Wilf ordered their drinks. He expected this child of nature to ask for soda water, but she surprised him.

"I'll have a margarita, please," she said.

As soon as they were served, he looked at her with a steady gaze, not angry, but firm. "What was tonight all about, Sage?" he asked.

She shrugged. "Just being neighborly."

"Being neighborly, or making fun of me?" he asked bluntly. "You didn't mention bringing your chaperon."

She had sensed upon first meeting him that he wasn't the kind of man you could push too far. "I guess maybe I was having a little joke," she admitted. "May and I had planned to go to the social. I couldn't cancel on her."

"There was some talk of a chicken in the oven when we first met."

"Yes, but I didn't say we were going to eat it tonight," she pointed out.

"You'll admit it was misleading, though," he insisted.

She nodded. "Guilty, as charged."

"As to bringing your chaperon!"

"My chaperon's not here now," she said with an encouraging look.

"That's good. I hoped maybe we could talk."

His mood told her he meant talk about the farm, and she admitted to herself that she was disappointed. She had been looking forward to an evening with a handsome, interesting man—getting to know him. "Yes. What is it you mean to build, Wilf?"

"Like I said, I can't reveal that. For professional reasons. But it isn't residential or industrial. Nothing that would destroy the character of the area."

"Recreational, then," she said much too quickly to please him. Her dreamy look had vanished long ago. Now it was replaced by one of keen intelligence.

"I guess you could call it that."

"A health farm, a riding stable, what?" He just shook his head, more in annoyance than disagreement. "A golf club," she said, and knew by his involuntary start that she had guessed right. "Don't worry, I won't tell anyone," she said. "It's not a bad idea. Hey, I'm not a nimby. I don't care if you build it in my backyard, at Newton's farm. It wouldn't bother me. You already have an option on Newton's place."

"Newton doesn't have enough land."

She thought a moment, then said, "There are lots of other farms in this area that might be glad to sell."

"I've canvassed the area pretty thoroughly. Your terrain is the most suitable."

"That's how you come to know Herman Hooten," she said.

If this woman was so sharp, he should be able to make her see the advantages to the deal he was offering her. He talked persuasively.

"You can't possibly be making any fortune on your herbs, Sage. I wish you'd reconsider. I'd be glad to help you scout out another location."

"That farm's my home, Wilf. My grandfather lived there, and his father before him. It's my legacy."

"How about your own father?" he asked, as she hadn't mentioned him.

"He was raised there, but he wasn't interested in farming. He's a businessman," she said vaguely. "And about finding me another farm, you have no idea how much work went into choosing just the right spot for everything. Herbs are living things, you know. They have needs—the right soil, the right amount of sun or shade. You can't just yank them up and put them anywhere."

"I might be able to talk my partner into raising the price," he said, peering at her from under lowered lashes.

She just shook her head. "You've been in the city too long. There's no truth to the rumor that everyone has his price."

He slowly lifted his head. Sage felt a spurt of annoyance to see he was smiling. "You still haven't heard my final price," he said.

Exasperated, she replied angrily, "I'm trying to be straight with you, Mr. Jameson."

"That's Wilf."

"Wilf. I don't intend to sell. You're just wasting your time here. Go back and have Herman fly you in some other direction. My farm can't be the only suitable location for your golf course."

"No, not the only, but the best. I always insist on the best."

She gave a sniff. "Then I'll give you the best advice I can. You're wasting your time. Go back to the drawing board. I wouldn't sell my farm for a million dollars, and I mean that. I'd never sell it."

His dark eyes studied her for a moment before he replied. "Never is a long time, Sage."

"You're hopeless!"

"On the contrary, I'm still hopeful you'll see reason."

She set down her drink and stood up. "Good night, and goodbye. Thanks for the drink."

He rose politely to his feet. "I'll see you around, Sage." She glared. "It's your turn to say, 'Not if I see you first, Mr. Jameson.' Don't forget the 'Mr. Jameson.' That adds the final touch of irritation to your temporary refusal."

"My refusal is *not* temporary."

"Then why are you so nervous? *I* think you're tempted. But a million is a little high. My partner'd never go for it. He's a hardheaded businessman." He smiled, thinking what a poor description this was of Ken Carson.

"If his head is any harder than yours, it must be made of granite."

"More like wood."

"Good night, again, Mr. Jameson."

She picked up her purse and flounced out.

Wilf ordered another ale and nursed it slowly. He hadn't been joking when he told Sage she was tempted. Anyone would be tempted by a million dollars. It was an inordinate price, of course. He had no intention of going that high, but in the worst case, it would still be a good investment.

Golf courses were very profitable, if they were run well. Then, too, they led to other profitable ventures—hotels, shops, housing. It didn't occur to him that this was contrary to what he'd told Sage about the project being purely recreational. His mind was just running in its habitual paths.

If it had occurred to him, he would have rationalized that those plans were long-range. The land near cities was bound to be developed eventually. Everyone wanted money. She'd be far better off if she sold. It must be some misguided sense of loyalty to her ancestors that made her so stubborn. Either that, or she planned to screw up the price by pretending she'd never sell. She might be a nature girl, but she was no dummy.

The thing to do was stick around for a few days. There was nothing needing his immediate attention at the office, and there was plenty of work to be done. He'd have to consult with the town officials about by-laws and that sort of thing. There were building permits to look into, and the water table. The greens needed plenty of water. Eventually a better road would be required. Time to begin making some friends at City Hall. She'd sell. It would take more than a few sprigs of parsley and thyme to stop him.

At home, Sage went to her office to review her column. She caught sight of herself in the mirror on the far wall, and was struck by the incongruence of her appearance. Her flowery dress and romantic hairdo were out of place in this office. She'd look more at home at a garden party, or dancing with a handsome man. Odd, Wilf hadn't suggested they dance at the bar. He hadn't seemed to notice her as a woman, which caused a sting of resentment.

Sage twitched the thought away and picked up her article on chamomile, one of her favorite herbs. She could almost smell its clovelike fragrance as she worked. It had been dedicated to the gods by the Egyptians, and was also a Saxon sacred herb. It was used for everything from serving as a lawn at Buckingham Palace to its cosmetic use to acting as a sleeping draft. And it was also good for the neighboring plants as it enriched the soil.

Since an interest in herbs seemed to be growing in the land, she had high hopes that a bigger chain might soon give her a nibble, and she wanted to make her writing good enough for a wider audience. Maybe she should look into getting an agent. She'd need one for her book when it was ready to sell in any case. Her accounting told her that she grossed more from her writing than from her farming and retail but it was her status as a professional grower that lent authority to her writing.

Her column was broadly based. She wrote about the origins and history of the plants, their traditional uses in the healing arts and cuisine as well as giving tips on growing them.

Sage worked until ten, then relaxed with some music and a cup of chamomile tea that acted as a soporific. May came home at ten-thirty with a pink teddy bear.

"This thing ended up costing me fifteen dollars," she grumbled. "I could have bought it for ten, but it's for a good cause I suppose."

"A new roof for the vicarage," Sage said.

"How did your evening with Wilf go?"

"He spent the whole time trying to convince me to sell the farm."

"The man must have rocks in his head. A pretty girl like you..."

Sage felt again that sting of annoyance, and realized that most of her anger with Wilf Jameson was his total lack of interest in her as a woman. Had she become so dowdy that she couldn't capture the interest of a man such as Wilf? She pushed the thought away—what did she want with a mercenary workaholic anyway?

She was well rid of that kind of man. Yet she realized that she wasn't interested in any of the local men, either. At times she thought she must have a split personality. Or maybe it was a love-hate relationship with big business and powerful businessmen.

"Let's watch the news," she said to avert one of May's pointed discussions on the pleasures of marriage.

When the phone rang at ten o'clock the next morning, Sage realized she was only fooling herself by pretending she wasn't interested in Wilf. Her heart thumped heavily when she lifted the receiver and heard the arrogant tone of his voice.

"Good morning, Sage. It's Wilf here. I'd like to repay last night's hospitality by taking you to dinner tonight if you're free."

He certainly didn't waste any time on small talk! "Just let me see if I'm tied up," she said. But it wasn't really necessary to check her calendar. She was free most evenings. That was when she usually did her writing. "Yes, tonight's fine," she said.

"I'll pick you up around seven-thirty."

"I'll see you then."

It was one of the shortest phone calls she'd had in years. He didn't inquire about her, or say why he was still in town. In fact, it reminded her of the stressed business calls of her working days. Wilf was probably rushing off to some meeting, but he had taken time to ensure he'd be with her that evening, and that was all that mattered to her.

Her mind was preoccupied by the date as she went through the motions of her day. Tonight she'd wear something special, to show Wilf she wasn't strictly a country mouse. She had a feeling that an evening with him would be a little out of the ordinary, and that meant going beyond Sanville. He'd mentioned Herman Hooten's helicopter. Maybe he'd hire it and fly them off to the city.

She began her preparations at six-thirty, and went to a lot of trouble to look especially attractive. She washed and blow-dried her hair in a seemingly casual way that took half an hour. Then she carefully applied evening makeup, and slipped into a killer black dress with a slim skirt and an open back. The dress demanded high heels. At the last minute, she dabbed perfume behind her ears and on her wrists.

She hadn't gone to this much trouble to look good since she'd turned farmer. But it was fun to do it for a special occasion, and a special man.

Wilf, however, spent part of his afternoon planning an outing to impress Sage. She liked simple, country things. It was difficult to arrange an outing to please her when he was a relative stranger to the area, staying at a hotel. He decided to rent a canoe and row to a nearby island for a cookout.

He'd bought steaks, large T-bones selected by himself, and had the butcher season them. Then he'd gone to a delicatessen to buy crusty rolls and a tossed salad. A bottle of very good burgundy—that she probably wouldn't appreciate—would accompany the steak. For dessert, he'd bought a bag of succulent green grapes and

Brie. A second thought told him she might not like the cheese, although he was certain she would enjoy the marshmallows to toast after. At the last minute, he'd even remembered to borrow dishes, cutlery and glasses from the hotel. The chef lent him a big wicker basket to hold his supplies.

At seven-thirty, he arrived in a T-shirt, blue jeans and sneakers, to find Sage waiting in a slinky black dress and high heels. They just stood a moment, staring at each other in dismay.

"I thought..." Sage came to an awkward pause.

"I rented a canoe. I thought a cookout... steaks..." *Oh Lord, I've goofed, but good!*

"Oh. That sounds lovely." She looked down at her dress and shoes. "Maybe I should change."

Wilf looked at them, too, and didn't want her to change. She looked exquisite in that clinging black dress that hugged her tiny waist. "Or we could go to a restaurant," he said.

"No, that's fine."

"But you're all dressed up."

"I'll change," she said, giving him a rather strange disappointed look, and went upstairs.

Chapter Three

When Sage had left, May said, to smooth the water, "Don't feel badly, Wilf. Sage really likes cookouts. We barbecue in the backyard all the time. It's just that she thought you might take her to a nice restaurant."

"I guess I really made a blunder, huh?"

"Try Aiken Island," May said. "There won't be anyone there. Nice and private. Can I get you a drink while you wait, Wilf? I'd stay and keep you company, but I've lost my cat. Whiskers hasn't been seen or heard from since two o'clock. I'm afraid he may have run into trouble."

"Go right ahead. I'm fine," he said.

She left, and was back in two minutes. "He's got up the pear tree again and is afraid to come down," she announced. "He goes chasing after a black squirrel. I'll have to get out the ladder."

"Let me help," he said, and went out with her.

She took him around to the pear tree in the backyard, where a ginger cat crouched on a low branch, mewing his discontent.

"He's such a chicken," she complained. "An ordinary cat would leap down, but not Whiskers." She tried to entice him to jump into her arms, but Whiskers just cringed and mewed. "I'll get the ladder," she said.

"I don't think we need one," Wilf said, and scrambled up the tree as easily as if it were a staircase. He cradled Whiskers in one arm and handed him down to May.

"You should be ashamed of yourself," she scolded Whiskers.

"Don't be too hard on him." Wilf smiled, stroking his head. "Maybe he has acrophobia."

May looked interested. "Well, now, maybe he has. He's even afraid to stand on the refrigerator. I put him there once, and he clung to me like a baby. I've heard of cat psychiatrists, so they must have neuroses like people. Thanks for the tip, Wilf."

"There's more to animals than we realize," he said, and told her about a friend whose dog was afraid of mice, as they returned to the living room.

In her room, Sage paced a moment, trying to decide what tack to take vis-à-vis Wilf. Had he chosen this outing as revenge for last night's social? Or did he think she'd enjoy roughing it? It was impossible to know, but it was rude to break a date, so she decided to go along with it. She quickly changed into jeans, a fleecy shirt and sneakers, knowing from experience that it could be chilly on the water at night.

Her smile was a little tense when she rejoined him. She was surprised to find Whiskers on his knee. "All set," she said. Then she added over her shoulder to May, "I see Whiskers showed up. Where was he?"

"Up the pear tree. Wilf rescued him. We discovered he has acrophobia. We've been discussing it, and think it stems from the time he was caught on the attic roof. You remember that's where I first found Whiskers, howling on the attic roof of the vicarage. They didn't know how he'd gotten there, poor thing."

She took the cat and thanked Wilf again.

"I won't be late, May," Sage said as they left.

May winked behind her back at Wilf. "You don't have to rush home on my account, Sage. I'll be out playing bridge until all hours."

Sage was glad she hadn't gone into a childish sulk, because Wilf seemed genuinely sorry about the misunderstanding. "I should have told you what I had in mind," he said. "In fact, I should have asked you what you'd like. It looks as if I've gone to a lot of trouble arranging an outing you don't much care for."

She realized it must have been difficult for him to concoct this picnic, and said, "That's all right. Just a misunderstanding. It'll be fun. Did I hear you mention steaks?"

"You don't eat red meat!" he exclaimed.

She laughed at his chagrined expression. "Don't be silly. Of course I eat steak, when I can afford it. What kind did you get?"

"T-bone."

"My favorite!"

"Mine, too. I like them rare."

"I like mine medium. We'll put mine on the fire first so they'll be done at the same time. Did you remember knives and forks?"

"I don't think I forgot anything," he said with a worried frown.

That frown convinced her he cared about this date, too, even if they had gotten their wires crossed about what sort of date it would be. "You've gone to a lot of trouble, Wilf. I appreciate it."

"I even brought marshmallows," he said, expanding under her admiration.

They drove to the dock. The canoe was already in the water. Sage soon got the idea that Wilf wasn't a boat man. He nearly tipped it as he got in, and when he took up the paddle, he paddled hard but awkwardly. It didn't really matter, as the canoe was still tied up.

"I'll get the line," she said, and untied it.

Wilf already regretted the outing he'd chosen. He liked powerboats and yachts, but this was his first time in a canoe, and it wasn't as easy as it looked.

He began paddling furiously, out into the middle of the channel. "What island did you have in mind?" she asked.

"Your aunt mentioned Aiken Island."

"It's that way," she said, pointing to the right. Leave it to May to choose an isolated island. There was an island nearby that was a state park with facilities for campers, but it was usually busy in the summer. Sage decided it might be more romantic to be alone with Wilf.

"Just getting the feel of the oars," he said to cover his embarrassment.

"That's paddle," she corrected.

As he was having so much trouble steering a straight course, Sage took up the other paddle and tried to counterbalance his meanderings. The island was not far, but it seemed an eternity to Wilf before they reached it.

He was in good shape from tennis and racquetball, but paddling used a different set of muscles. He knew he'd be stiff by morning.

Hopeful that he would have convinced Sage to sell, Wilf remained in good humor. It was darned nice of her not to sulk at having to change her attire. He decided she was equally attractive in closely fitting jeans. Her evening makeup and hairdo made even jeans and sneakers look glamorous.

Once he got the rhythm of the paddle, he began to enjoy it. The breeze cooled his heated brow, and the view was marvelous. The setting sun cast a net of gold and crimson over the water. In the distance the towering trees looked black against the sky. It made him feel like a kid again, playing Robinson Crusoe.

He hopped out as soon as they landed and helped Sage out of the canoe. "Now we'll gather some driftwood," he said, rubbing his hands in a businesslike way.

"Hadn't we better haul the canoe up first? It's starting to drift."

Wilf looked in alarm, and saw it had already drifted a few feet from shore. He barged into the water, and sank to his ankles. The water felt like ice as it penetrated his shoes and socks.

"We'll put your socks and shoes by the fire to dry out as soon as we've collected our wood," Sage said. She managed not to shake her head, but she had a pretty good idea which of them would have to make the fire, and probably cook the steaks, too.

"Now to gather some driftwood," Wilf said, looking around for this commodity.

There wasn't so much as a splinter to be seen.

Sage pointed to a pile of rocks arranged in a makeshift barbecue pit. "Others have been here before us and used the wood up," she said. "At least we won't have to build a pit. We'll have to go into the bush a bit. We'd better do it, before it gets dark."

She was thankful for her long sleeves. The thorns from a patch of raspberry bushes pulled at her shirt. "Be careful," she called as Wilf felt a thorn yank the skin from his forearm. That was only a minor sting. The real discomfort was his soaking feet. His sneakers emitted a squelching sound at every step.

They found a tree that had fallen some years before. The branches were denuded and dry enough that they could break off the smaller ones. Here, at last, Wilf could show his masculine strength. Loud cracks rent the air as he pulled the wood free. They both took an armload to the pit and piled it in.

"Now we'll light the fire," he said with an anticipatory smile.

Sage stared at him as if he were mad. "This isn't enough to cook a steak," she told him. "You have to keep replenishing it, or find some big logs to put on top. This is just kindling, to get it started. And with the marshmallows for later, we'll need four or five times this much."

"Oh! Yes, of course. Back into the bushes."

The only big wood was the fallen tree, and as they couldn't drag it to their fire, they made several trips. When Sage decided they had enough, she said, "Now for some paper to put under the wood to get it started."

"Paper?"

"Kindling will do," she said, and began poking the smallest branches under the larger pieces. "You did bring matches?"

Wilf had remembered to grab a match flap from the Belview, and took it from his pocket. He was tired and ravenous, and his feet felt like two blocks of ice. He wouldn't have minded that so much, but he knew he had made a poor appearance in front of Sage.

The fire was slow to take, but eventually a weak flame flickered and he got the steaks out of the basket. It occurred to him that you couldn't just throw meat on the wood. He should have brought some sort of grate. His masculine pride objected to seeking a woman's help. He had already shown himself as incapable, but try as he might, he couldn't think of anything to use for a grate.

Sage was conjuring the same problem, and had found the solution. The last people to use the pit had left behind a round grate from a small backyard barbecue. She arranged it over the fire. It was too much to hope that Wilf had brought a long-handled fork. They'd just have to fling the steaks onto the grate, and rescue them later with a stick as best they could.

Wilf breathed a sigh of relief when he saw that grate. "Why don't you set out the fixings while I cook the steaks?" he suggested.

She was pleasantly surprised to find plates, knives, forks, and even paper napkins in the basket. She arranged them on a table rock and went to watch the steaks cook. Wilf had remembered to put hers on first. The tantalizing aroma of sizzling beef made her realize that she was ravenous.

"I'll turn yours and put mine on now," Wilf said.

The flames were leaping high by this time, and he realized that turning Sage's steak would involve barbecued fingers if he didn't find a turning tool.

Seeing his problem, she said, "I'll find a sharp branch."

Even a sharp branch didn't penetrate the meat easily, but eventually Wilf got it flipped, with only a little ash on one end. When the steaks were both done, Sage suggested he put his shoes and socks near the pit to dry. She put the steaks on the plates and took them to the table rock while he did this. He soon limped forward.

"Come on tenderfoot, the food's getting cold." She grinned.

They both looked for salt simultaneously. "I forgot the salt!" he howled. "Doggonit! I wanted everything to be perfect."

"Salt's not good for you, anyway, Wilf. More importantly, did you bring a corkscrew for that French burgundy? I want to compliment you on your choice, by the way."

He was a little surprised that she appreciated the vintage, but of course he couldn't say so. "Yes, I have a corkscrew," he said, and produced one with a plastic handle heralding the Belview. After a struggle, he got the cork out and filled their glasses.

They touched rims and tasted the wine. "Perfect," she sighed. "I haven't had wine like this since—for ages." Not since her days with Baxter and Associates, wooing clients at fancy restaurants. It seemed aeons ago.

This was much nicer, dining under the indigo sky, with a few stars peeping out, and a fat white moon adding an artistic touch. The wind whispered through the tall pines, and the breeze from the river mingled with the scent of pine resin.

"How'd you come to get into this business, Wilf?" she asked.

"My dad was a postman. I didn't get to college. I always knew I was interested in business, though. After wasting a few years behind a counter at a bank, I became bored counting other people's money. I became a real estate salesman, and soon realized the money was in developing. I saved up my money and found a small town just howling for a mall. I rounded up partners and built it. One thing led to another. That was ten years ago. Along the way, my cousin came into money, and entered into a partnership with me."

"Now you're building golf resorts," she said, urging him on.

"Yes, in addition to hotels and those apartment towers you love to hate."

"Do you do all your building in the States?"

"We branched out five years ago, beginning with a luxury hotel in Cancun. Most of our development is in North America, but we've done quite a bit in the Caribbean. Now with east Europe to be developed, we'll be looking in that direction. And, of course, the Persian Gulf will need a lot of building, too."

Sage felt a surge of nostalgia for her former life. All this sounded so exciting, hopping planes to far-off countries, arranging deals. Sometimes she missed the excitement.

"You make it sound easy, but it must have been exhausting. I imagine it's hard to raise money for those huge projects."

"It was at the beginning, but I've paid my dues. Now that I have a good track record, the moneymen treat me with respect."

"Paid my dues...track record." Sage could think she was back at Baxter's. That soon reminded her of the other side of the fast track.

"Don't you ever get the urge to just drop it all and enjoy life? You must be rich by now. Why kill yourself?"

"I guess I'm one of those people who believe in the work ethic," he said.

Sage felt a tingle of annoyance at this patronizing speech. Was he implying she was shiftless, content to fritter her life away? "If that's a dig at my life-style, I'll have you know farming is no breeze."

"I know it's hard and unprofitable. That's why I can't understand your refusal to sell. You'd be miles ahead financially."

She gave a wistful look at the romantic surroundings. Wilf seemed immune to them; he was only interested in business. "Like I said, money's not everything." She shrugged.

"No, but it buys everything." He filled her glass.

"I don't want a lot of things—you know, clothes and fancy cars and jewelry. The ultimate luxury is time. It seems to me my city friends are always trying to buy time. They pay people to do their housework and shopping and look after their kids. They're working to buy other people's time. They don't have any time to themselves, to just relax and enjoy life."

"But you work hard on your farm, growing those herbs."

"That's different. I like it. Heck, I was doing it just for fun before I made a business out of it. I was giving my wares away to the neighbors."

"I like what I'm doing, too," he said. "I'm not just in it for the money. It gives me a sense of satisfaction to drive around the country, seeing projects I built. Good, useful projects that enhance the quality of people's lives."

He brought out the bag of grapes, and while they nibbled, he spoke with passion about various projects he'd developed. He had won awards from the industry, and been given the keys to various cities by grateful town councils. Sage admired his energy and drive.

She had always responded to that passion and conviction in a man. She used to have that same ambitious streak herself, but she had overdone it and burned out. Or maybe her whole heart had never been in it. She was beginning to realize the financial insecurity of her childhood had had something to do with it. She wanted other things, too. She was eventually convinced that Wilf wasn't just a money-grubbing developer, but she didn't change her mind about selling him her farm.

"You've found your calling, and I've found mine," she said when he'd stopped. "And now let's toast those marshmallows before the fire goes out."

They found sharpened branches to use as skewers for the marshmallows. The wine induced a feeling of languor, and the dancing flames colored the moments with romance. Across the flickering light, Sage examined the rugged planes of Wilf's face. It was all angles, from the slash of eyebrows to the lean cheeks and squared chin. She responded viscerally to the masculine strength of it. In fact, she had never met anyone so downright sexy. Sage had heard that power was an aphrodisiac, but power alone wasn't enough. Her former boss Mike Baxter was powerful, and she despised him.

A man needed integrity, as well, before she could care for him. From what he had said, she sensed that Wilf had integrity. He didn't boast of profitable deals; he seemed concerned that his development projects were useful and well constructed. He was a genuinely nice man.

Of course, he was hopelessly out of his element in the wilds like this. She would like to see him in his own milieu, where his strengths showed. He would be a strong, take-charge businessman. He had to be, to have made such a brilliant career with no special academic training.

Wilf sensed her softening mood, and moved closer to her. When his marshmallow was done, he pulled it from the stick and held it up to her mouth. "Be careful, it's hot!" he warned. At close range, he noticed the ripe fullness of her lips and the liquid glow of her eyes in the firelight. He'd better be careful, too!

"I'll let it cool a minute," she said. When their eyes met, a sense of awareness hung about them. Sage felt that he was acutely conscious of her as a woman, as she was conscious of his masculinity.

He set the marshmallow down and put an arm companionably around her shoulder. "Do you want to sing some golden oldies?" he suggested, to lighten the building mood.

She relaxed against him, enjoying the warm strength of his chest. She felt by this time that there was no fear of his becoming aggressively amorous. They'd been on the island for two hours, and he hadn't made any objectionable moves. His arm tightened, and she looked up. "Bridge Over Troubled Water, you mean? If I Had a Hammer? You choose."

Moonlight turned her hair to silver and reflected in her eyes, while flickering shadows from the fire animated her face. Wilf felt a pronounced frustration. He had rules about romancing clients or clients-to-be, but this night seemed made for a little romance. One kiss couldn't do any harm.

Sage knew by the way Wilf was gazing at her, every atom of his body tense, that he had forgotten all about singing. He was going to kiss her, and her heart hammered at the thought as his head lowered slowly, inevitably, to hers.

His lips brushed hers in a slow, tantalizing taste, gentle as a breeze, before they firmed. Then his arms swept around her, pulling her closely against him. She felt a sharp surge of excitement as the thrust of her breasts yielded to his firmer muscle. She felt suddenly vulnerable, but there was no menace in one kiss. Her alarm subsided to pleasure, and a feeling of contentment washed over her.

Sage wondered whether the wine, or the cozy fire, or the starry sky was to blame for the feeling of security. Or was it being ensconced by Wilf's warm embrace, holding her safe and warm while the kiss deepened? She wouldn't let it get out of hand. She'd just savor the delight of the moment. Now she should—but not quite yet. He began stroking her lips provocatively with his tongue, and she moved in protest—or was it encouragement? It did feel awfully nice. Nice and sexy.

Something inside her began to melt. She shouldn't let him put his hand there! Well, maybe as long as he didn't move it. Oh but he was moving it in slow, persuasive strokes that ravished her senses to a golden glow.

She meant to stop him when she lifted her hand, but suddenly her fingers were reveling in his crisp black hair, drawing his head closer for a harder kiss. When Wilf's hand began stealing under her shirt, she shook herself to attention and drew reluctantly away.

"I guess that marshmallow will be cooled down by now," she said in a breathless voice that betrayed her agitation.

"The marshmallow might," he said in a dazed voice, gazing softly at her.

He popped it into her mouth. "Perfect!" She finished it before speaking again. "It's been a lovely evening, Wilf."

"No, it's been a fiasco—until now." He drew her head back to his shoulder and ran his fingers through her silken hair, but didn't try to resume their lovemaking. "I'm sorry I foisted this picnic idea on you, Sage. You've been a real trooper. I racked my brain to think of something you'd enjoy. Something simple—bucolic I mean. That's not a slur on your intelligence."

"Of course," she said, but as she considered it, she wasn't so sure she wanted him to think of her as a simple country girl. This was a man she could get serious about. She had encouraged Wilf to do most of the talking, with the result that he hadn't learned much about her. She thought that perhaps she should open up a little. She'd tell him about her past, and how she had worked hard, like him, to better herself.

"This reminds me of my childhood," she said, pushing another marshmallow on her stick. "My parents lived in a commune when I was small. I guess you'd call them hippies."

Wilf nodded, obviously interested. "I had that feeling when I met you. There was something uniquely sixties about you. An experience like that leaves its mark. I imagine that's why you don't have much interest in worldly things. But the hippie movement soon petered out, Sage. People can't live in the past, existing on roots and love. Flower power. You have to grow beyond that."

She stiffened perceptibly. So he thought she was a shiftless, ambitionless throwback to the past! Without even waiting to hear what she had to say, he was reading her a lecture. "I don't live in the past, exactly," she said through thin lips. "I expect what you really mean is that I should sell my farm to you and rent a stall in one of your malls."

"What a great idea!" he laughed. "Are you coming to see the light?"

"How often do I have to tell you I'm not interested!"

She stood up and marched to the lake. Naturally this city slicker hadn't brought anything to douse the fire. Sage picked up the wine bottle and filled it with water to douse the fire. It took a couple of trips, during which Wilf first pulled on his still damp but now steaming socks and shoes, then began to pack up their dishes and refuse.

"Let's go," she said, with a last look around to check to see if they had forgotten anything.

Wilf was sorry to see the evening end on such a sour note. It was bad for business, and beyond that, he was sorry he'd offended her, because he found Sage Cramer a charming woman. He put his hand on her elbow. "Sage, if I said something to offend you, I'm sorry. Doing so was the furthest thing from my mind. Everything was going so well. What did I do?"

"How could you criticize me when you don't know anything about me, and apparently aren't interested in hearing what I have to say?" she retorted.

He looked puzzled. "What do you mean?"

"You failed, Mr. Jameson. Probably a first for you. You only came here to try to talk me into selling, but my mind is made up. I'll ne—"

He lifted a finger and placed it on her lips. "Don't say it. Give me another chance."

He was smiling, which was the last straw. Without another word, Sage strode off to the canoe, lifted it from the bank, and got in, wetting her feet in the process. She took what satisfaction she could from seeing Wilf do the same thing. Conversation was practically nonexistent on the trip home. Sage thanked him coolly at the door, said good-night, and went inside.

Chapter Four

"How did it go last night?" May asked eagerly over breakfast the next morning.

"Wilf tried to talk me into selling. I told him I wasn't interested. End of Wilf Jameson," Sage said flippantly, but there was an angry edge to her voice. That was the way she had decided to look at it. He had just been trying to sweet talk her into selling, and she wasn't green enough to fall for that. She poured a cup of foul-looking coffee and buttered a bran muffin.

"And he seemed so nice, rescuing Whiskers and everything. I'd hoped you had found someone at last."

"You make me sound like Mrs. Methuselah, May. So how was your evening?" she said hurriedly to change the subject. May could usually be diverted by talk of her bridge game.

"I had the worst hands I've ever held in my life," she replied, and went on with details while Sage munched her muffin. "I'm thinking of taking up crocheting. It'd be cheaper. I lost ten bucks. What are you up to this morning?"

"It's time to harvest the first cuttings of chervil and parsley, maybe some basil, too. They're promised to the supermarket for today. I'll be overseeing the operation."

Sage had to keep an eye on the high school students she'd hired to do these jobs, especially while they were learning about gardening and agriculture. "I'm going to prune the angelica, too. It gets leggy if you don't pinch it back. Where's Whiskers today?" she asked, looking around.

"On the porch, looking for Mr. Squirrel. You don't think Wilf might drop around to say goodbye?" she asked, squinting at Sage's old clothes.

She had to dress for her job, usually in jeans, a T-shirt and sneakers as she wore that morning. "I don't think so," Sage said, and left. On her way out the back door, she picked up a blue denim hat to keep the sun off her head and out of her eyes.

She enjoyed working among her plants. The air was sweeter than perfume. After she had explained the job to the students, she worked alongside them for a while to watch and advise them. As she cut the basil, she remembered things she had read. Everyone loved basil on tomatoes and in cooking, but it had other less known uses that were untapped. Made into a drink, it was excellent for settling the stomach of pregnant women, and with no dangerous side effects. That was the sort of information she liked to introduce to her reading audience.

Parsley was another underutilized herb. It usually ended up on the side of the plate after being used as a decoration. A waste of good vitamins and iron. It made a terrific tonic, and the crushed leaves were good against insect bites. She also warned parrot owners to keep it away from their birds as it could be fatal to them.

At ten-thirty she went into the house for a glass of water, and saw a florist's box on the table. May was hacking at carrots and a carcass of chicken, which threatened one of her soups for lunch.

"Who sent you flowers?" Sage asked. "Is it your bridge partner, apologizing for last night?"

"They're for you," May said, shoving the box toward her and peering to see the card.

"For me!" Sage tore open the box, as excited as a kid. "I bet they're from Mike Baxter. He tries to lure me back from time to time."

"Looks like a local beau. The delivery was made by Vandentops, florists in Sanville."

Sage drew back the green paper and emitted a soft "Oo-oh!" of pleasure. Two dozen furled red roses nestled amid the delicate greenery of fern. She lifted the card, her mind already darting to Wilf Jameson. This didn't seem like him.

"I'm sorry about last night. Let me make it up, and I'll give you a dinner worthy of that black dress. Hopefully yours, Wilf."

A soft smile tugged at her lips. That was rather sweet of him. While she arranged the roses in a crystal vase, she wondered whether she'd accept his offer. He knew now that she definitely wasn't going to sell her farm, so if he still wanted to see her, maybe his interest was becoming more personal. She still wanted to let him know something about her true background, because she sensed that he wouldn't be satisfied with some naive woman who didn't understand his life-style. She had been a little sharp with him last night, and after all, he had made a good effort to entertain her.

She'd see him, but it was her turn to entertain again, and she'd do it in style. She'd serve him a gourmet meal that let him know she was a sophisticated, urban woman, even if she did live on a farm.

There was a phone in the kitchen, but she went into her office to call. This conversation might just possibly require privacy.

"Wilf Jameson here," he said crisply when the switchboard put her through.

"It's Sage Cramer. I was afraid you might be out. I received the roses. They're lovely, Wilf. Thank you."

"I'm glad you like them, but more importantly, did you get my card?"

"Yes. I'd love to have dinner with you. Why don't you come here? I'll make you a home-cooked meal."

Wilf was a little disappointed. He had nothing against home cooking, but he knew the aunt would be there, and that wasn't the sort of evening he had hoped for.

"That sounds great," he said, trying to inject a little enthusiasm into his reply. "Maybe we can do something after—go to a show, or for a drive." He didn't like to say "be alone," but she read between the lines.

"We'll see," she replied encouragingly.

"I don't want to make any mistakes this time, Sage. What do I wear? I mean, if you're planning to show me how a barbecue *should* be conducted..."

"I'll be wearing a long dress," she said, to intrigue him, and to give him a hint as to what he should wear. "But don't feel you have to dash out and buy a black tie."

She wasn't too happy with his laugh. It suggested that she wouldn't know a black tie from a hair ribbon.

"Fortunately I have a spare pair of pants, so I won't have to show up in the ones that kid spilt his drink on at that fair the other night."

"Good. We'll try not to overwhelm you all at once. Shall we say eightish, to have time for a drink first?"

Again he was surprised. Dining at city hours? The strawberry social had started at six. "See you then. I look forward to it."

"Bye."

She ran out to the kitchen. "Wilf's coming here for dinner, May. I want you to invite someone to even up the table. Maybe Hal Jenkins," she suggested.

Hal was the dean of English at the university in Buffalo, and one of May's suitors. It was a constant surprise to Sage that so many men were interested in May. Hal spent the summers on his hobby farm nearby, usually working on articles for the academic press. He was an amusing, civilized man. Sage was determined to show Wilf Jameson she was used to being surrounded by cultured, sophisticated people.

"What do you want me to prepare?" May asked.

"I'll do the cooking tonight."

May gave her a knowing look. "You must be serious about this Wilf, if you're not willing to subject him to my burnt offerings."

"Don't be silly," Sage said, embarrassed. "You know I often cook when I want to try out new recipes. I thought I'd start with my herb broth, and serve rosemary chicken for the main dish. There are some baby carrots ready to pick. I'll finish them in butter and mint leaves."

"And your pilaf, I suppose."

"I got a lot of letters congratulating me on that recipe. Yes, the herb pilaf. I'll have to go to Sanville after lunch."

"What for? We have all the fixings."

"We don't have any vermouth. Maybe I'll serve martinis first. I noticed a lot of people drinking them the last time I was in the city."

"He'll think you're an alcoholic."

"Who cares?" Sage shrugged, but her excitement belied the offhand remark.

"Obviously not you, or you wouldn't be going to all this trouble," May said with a knowing grin. "Since you're putting me out of the kitchen, I'll clean up the house."

"And if you wouldn't mind doing the table. I'd like to use Grandma's linen tablecloth and the good silver and dishes. And maybe a nice bouquet for a centerpiece." She looked at the roses, but decided their stems were too long. She'd put them on the side table in the living room.

"I'm glad you're not trying to impress him, or you'd run out and buy new furniture," May said.

"No, I wouldn't have time. I'm planning to get my hair done."

May just shook her head. "It's nice to see you interested in a man—at last."

"It's nice to be interested," Sage said musingly. She loved her work, but as she so often said herself, there was more to life than work.

The day was a busy pleasure, making her arrangements, picking fresh herbs and preparing dinner. Mouth-watering aromas wafted through the house as she simmered her herb broth and prepared the chicken breasts, rolled thin and filled with rosemary.

She looked for Wilf in Sanville, while running last-minute errands, but didn't see him. She wondered why he had remained in town. Perhaps he had taken her advice and was scouting some other location for his golf course. If he found a site, he'd be around town for a while. Or possibly he had remained in town just to see her...

She had the local hairdresser wash and blow her hair dry in a soft, wavy style. Since she had promised Wilf a long dress, she had to reach to the back of her closet, where her city clothes hung in plastic covers. She drew out a wispy silk so finely woven it felt like a cool mist against her skin. Pale flowers were splashed over a washed-out blue background. The gown had little shape except for the body beneath it. It flowed gracefully when she moved.

She had lost her easy expertise in applying evening makeup, but the old tricks slowly returned as she whisked on eye shadow and highlighted her cheeks with a pale skim of rose. She wanted one striking piece of jewelry, and selected a set of carved jade earrings that dangled nearly to her shoulders. They had been a gift from a satisfied Oriental customer. They picked up the green of her eyes, emphasizing the color.

May was still in her room when Sage went downstairs. Sage loved her grandparents' house, but its homey warmth wasn't the backdrop she wanted this evening. She decided to serve cocktails on the cedar deck that gave a view of her rolling hills.

A mist of heavenly scents blew in from her herb gardens. The smoky gray of sage and thyme provided a contrast to the dark green of parsley and basil. Hints of purple showed among the chives and mint. It was like nature's own patchwork quilt. Wilf would realize it was impossible to part with it when he saw it in all its summer glory.

In Sanville, Wilf had been equally concerned to make a good impression. He hadn't given up on acquiring the farm, but quite apart from that, he felt he had offended Sage in some manner, and wanted to atone for it. Since she appreciated good wine—again he'd wondered about that—he'd bought a bottle of Chablis, and tucked it under his arm as he strode up to her front door. He felt that eightish meant eight o'clock in the country, and not eight-thirty.

He smiled at the quaint wreath of dried flowers hanging on the door. A milk can painted wedgwood blue and filled with dried grass occupied one corner of the steps. He lifted the door knocker, an apple fashioned in brass, and tapped lightly.

Sage took a last look in the mirror before answering the door. "Oh, you're early!" she exclaimed to let him know she was familiar with more cosmopolitan social etiquette. Then she gave a carefree laugh. "I mean, you're on time. How nice."

Wilf stared at her, taking in the gown and hair and jewelry, and felt he was seeing a different woman than he'd expected. She looked even more elegant than she had last night in that black sheath. In fact, she looked as if she belonged on the pages of a glossy fashion magazine. Sage looked as if she wouldn't know which end of a spade to hold in her hand.

"You look lovely," he said.

"Why thank you. And thanks for the wine," she said, accepting the bottle, and setting it aside. "I thought we'd have a drink on the patio while waiting for Dr. Jenkins. He'll be joining us. My aunt will be right down."

He followed her through the homey parlor, catching the scent of her musky perfume as she moved. The room, at least, was more or less what he had been expecting. It seemed the appropriate background for the old Sage, but hardly suitable for this new one. On the patio, comfortable garden chairs were arranged along a cedar deck, with a drinks table set up on the side. Several bottles of liquor, an ice bucket and mix comprised the makeshift bar. She had gone to a lot of trouble.

"What would you like to drink?" she asked. "A martini? Scotch?"

"Scotch will be fine," he said, and walked to the railing to look out over the view. "What's that lovely smell, Sage?" he asked over his shoulder.

"I guess you could call it potpourri. It's the mingled scent of my herbs. It's always stronger in the evening. That's probably due to the breeze. It is lovely, isn't it?"

"Is that entire area of land where you grow your herbs?" he asked, gesturing to the fields beyond.

"Mmm-hmm. Did you think I only grew them in my little knot garden in front of the shop? That's just for show."

"I had no idea your operation was so extensive. It must be a labor-intensive operation."

"It is. Fortunately the busy season coincides with the school holidays, and the work isn't terribly demanding, except on the spine. It involves a lot of bending. I hire two dozen students."

"That many!"

"That's just for the maintenance and cuttings. I have people to help out with the drying and mixing and bottling and so on, as well. I have a sort of lab, out in what used to be the stable, where I test blends for bouquet garni, for cooking. Also drying techniques. And of course, the shop runs all year."

He shook his head, dazed. "I thought you just grew a little patch for your shop."

"No, I have quite an extensive mail-order business, as well. Dried mixtures of herbs, seeds and roots, of course, and all kinds of booklets."

Wilf was impressed, yet as he gazed into the distance, he noticed that the actual gardens weren't that extensive. "How many acres under cultivation?" he asked.

"Upward of ten. It's growing all the time."

That left a hundred and forty not being utilized. Maybe he could buy them, and let Sage keep her operation intact. It was so lovely and peaceful here, it did seem a shame to interfere with it.

"I'm impressed," he said when she brought him his drink. A breeze lifted her curls and molded her silken dress to her body. The curve of her breast brought a fleeting memory of that kiss by the fireside. "And not just with your operation either," he added in a burred voice as his eyes lingered on her, turning it into a personal compliment.

Sometimes silence is the best answer. Sage just gazed back at him, smiling enigmatically. She didn't reply in words, but he read an answering interest in her look. "Cheers," she said, still wearing that secret look, and touched her glass to his. He would have thought she was drinking water, except for the olive in the bottom of her glass. A martini? Sage Cramer? This woman was full of surprises.

"How long have you been doing this?" he asked, gesturing to her garden.

"Only two years. I used to work in the city, like you."

His eyebrows lifted in interest. "Maybe we have more in common than I thought," he said.

"Maybe we have," she answered.

"What did you do, in the city?"

"I worked for a business consultant firm."

Wilf was just about to ask her what she did at the firm when they were interrupted by the arrival of Dr. Hal Jenkins and May Cramer. He figured she must have been a secretary or receptionist. If she'd been an accounts executive she never would have thrown the job over. They made big bucks. Anyway, she looked too young for a top executive position.

Sage made the introduction. "Dr. Jenkins is the Dean of English at the university," she said, glancing to see if Wilf was impressed.

"Delighted to meet you, Doctor," Wilf said, shaking his hand.

"Call me Hal, please. You're not a local man, Wilf?"

"Wilf is a real estate developer," Sage explained.

Hal gave an exaggerated groan. "Don't destroy our lovely countryside, please."

"He's only looking for a place to build a golf course," Sage said hastily. She had forgotten Hal Jenkins was a die-hard environmentalist.

Sage didn't see the sharp look Wilf gave her. That was supposed to be a secret!

"Anyway, Hal, it was my acreage he had his eye on, not yours," she added.

"A golf course, eh?" Hal said, warming to the idea. "I wouldn't mind that. I have to drive ten miles, and even then the Pinewood course is inferior. Only nine holes, and with very little variation in the layout."

May brought Hal a Scotch and soda, and the men talked a little about golf. Sage felt guilty when she heard

Wilf telling Hal that the golf course was not public knowledge, and he'd appreciate it if he kept it quiet. "The competition, you know," he explained.

"I know just what you mean, Wilf. It's the same in my business. You come up with a good idea, someone hears about it and beats you to the punch. I was preparing a paper on Mrs. Eden. She's a lady you might not be familiar with—nineteenth-century English—a fine writer. Would you believe it, one of my colleagues, from a different college of course, saw her books on my desk and ran off behind my back to do an essay on her. All my research was in vain."

"I'm relieved to see you're in sympathy with my aim, Hal. I've done a lot of research myself. This area has real potential for a championship course. It would be a shame if some fly-by-night operator moved in on me and set up an inferior course."

"My lips are sealed," Hal said, and moved away to talk to May.

Wilf watched him with an air of concern as he left. "I hope he means that. It was supposed to be a secret," he reminded Sage.

Her hand flew to her lips. "I'm sorry!" she said. He could see she was upset. "I thought that since I won't sell, you'd given up the idea."

"I haven't given up."

"I'm sure you can rely on Hal. He's trustworthy. He doesn't have much to do with developers or local businessmen in any case. He comes here to get away from it all, you know. He spends most of his time writing. I promise I won't blab to anyone else."

"That's all right," he said. "Word usually does get out, one way or another."

They joined Hal and May, and began to talk about other things. "How's your writing coming along, Sage?" Hal asked.

"My column's been picked up by a syndicate," she announced proudly.

Wilf listened with eager curiosity. She hadn't said anything about writing.

Hal said, "Yes, I happened to be glancing through the *Lyndonville Herald* and saw it. Congratulations."

Wilf's curiosity dwindled. It was obviously some small town newspaper they were talking about. "What sort of column do you write, Sage?" he asked.

"I do a weekly article on my herbs," she said. "I'm compiling all my columns for a book that I hope to get published."

This was the hope of nine out of ten freelance journalists. Wilf didn't think it would come to anything, but he expressed polite interest.

"I particularly enjoyed your column on southernwood," Hal continued. "Some of that old folklore is amusing. Old Man's Love, you said it used to be called. Is that because it's considered a cure for baldness?"

"Actually the name is Old Man's or Lad's Love, so that can't be the meaning. I'm still following it up. One of my readers might know. It's used mostly as an ornamental plant now. They used to believe it was a safeguard against evil spirits and witches. It doesn't do well in our temperate climate. It prefers the warmth of southern France."

"Hence the name southernwood, no doubt," Hal said.

When they finished their drinks, Sage went into the kitchen to serve dinner and May led the men to the table. Wilf didn't know quite what to expect. He rather thought a homey roasted chicken and apple pie might be on the menu. He certainly hadn't expected this gracious table set with lavish silverware, fine china, crystal and a centerpiece of flowers.

He detected the tantalizing aroma of chicken simmering in herbs emanating from the kitchen. But first Sage served her herb broth with hot breads. It had a subtle taste. There was sherry in there somewhere. The bouquet lingered on the tongue, teasing memory.

With the rosemary chicken, she served her wine. The boneless breasts were stuffed with herbed dressing, and wine gravy with bits of onion and celery. The fowl had imbibed the savory flavors, which tantalized somewhat dormant olfactory senses. The baby carrots were cooked al dente, and finished off in butter and mint. Hal and Wilf were both impressed.

"You ought to open a restaurant," Hal said, as he said every time he dined with them.

"Maybe I'll write a recipe book instead," she replied. "The logistics of opening a restaurant aren't favorable. Neither is the carrying cost. It's too labor-intensive, too much overhead, and the opening costs are unreal. I prefer a simpler and more secure investment."

Wilf wondered just what, exactly, she had done for that consulting firm she'd mentioned. She seemed to have picked up a few pointers about business.

"That's your business background speaking." Hal laughed. "I think you mentioned you studied business at college?"

"Yes, and I worked as a management consultant for a few years," she added, ostensibly telling Hal, but wanting Wilf to hear it.

When she glanced at Wilf, he lifted his eyebrows in tacit acknowledgment that he'd underestimated her. "That seems an odd background for your present undertaking. Whatever made you decide to run a farm?" he asked. "Talk about a labor-intensive, insecure operation!"

"The difference is that I like it," she said briefly.

"A case of the heart ruling the head," Hal laughed.

"I wouldn't say that," Sage objected. "A case of the head and the heart working together. I'm not exactly going broke, you know."

Hal said, "If you ever skate near the edge, open a little restaurant. Or even a take-out meal service. You'll have a faithful customer in me."

"Are you hinting for a second helping, Hal?" May asked.

"Yes, I am," he said frankly.

Both men had seconds, which didn't deter them from enjoying their dessert of chocolate mousse, and their coffee. They took the coffee out to the patio, to enjoy with a glass of liqueur.

Hal leaned back in his chair and rambled on contentedly. "When I bought my little farm, I was afraid I'd spend my summers in a cultural or intellectual wasteland. It was a wonderful surprise to find such charming and diverse neighbors. Of course, in our age of instant communications, the world is a global village. There's really no such thing as what we used to call a provincial in this day and age. My country neighbors travel abroad every winter. They know Europe better than I do."

Sage said, "It's funny how the old stereotypes linger though." She felt Wilf's eyes on her and turned to meet his gaze. "Just because you live on a farm, people expect you to be a little out of touch."

"Funny how we try to live up to their expectations, too," Hal laughed. "I always drive my little pickup truck when I have my colleagues down to visit. I wear old clothes, and talk about 'the lower forty' as if I were a real farmer. I only have five acres," he explained to Wilf.

"Yes, I've noticed that tendency to play the role," Wilf replied blandly. He directed a speaking glance to Sage as he spoke.

She knew this remark was for her, and wondered if it were true. She hadn't consciously tried to mislead him. Well, perhaps taking him to the strawberry social had been a bit much, but the next night he was the one who had suggested the picnic.

"We all enjoy playing roles in life," Hal said, and continued in this vein for a while. He seemed to miss the lecture room, and was apt to crop out into a lecture at the drop of a hint.

A little later, Hal said to Sage, "You mentioned you had found a copy of John Gerard's book on herbs. I'd dearly love to have a glance at it, if it isn't too much trouble."

"It isn't an original sixteenth-century copy, of course," Sage said, "but it's old. And it has wonderful illustrations. I found it at a used bookstore. I'll get it."

"I always enjoy browsing among your old books. Will it be all right if I go with you?"

"Of course." Sage turned to Wilf. "Would you like to come along, Wilf?"

"I'll get us another cup of coffee," May said, rising. "Or maybe herbal tea would be better. We don't want to be awake all night."

Rather than sit alone, Wilf went with Sage and Hal. He didn't think he would have much to offer in a discussion of vintage books, but he was the sort of man who was always eager to listen and learn. He followed them through the house and into the office.

When Sage flicked on the lights, he blinked in surprise. He had been expecting another quaintly decorated room with a little cubbyhole desk and a typewriter wedged in one corner for writing her articles. He found himself gazing at all the latest technological wizardry. Fax machine, computer, separate word processor, printer with paper track, and a wall of filing cabinets.

She was obviously up to the minute in her business concerns, yet with all the electronics, she had managed to imbue the room with something of her own style and grace. The old prints on the wall and the soft green of the carpet underfoot removed the hard edge. Lacy plants softened the geometrical severity of the windows, and along one wall, the bookshelves had the pleasantly jumbled air of books that are read and not just serving as props in the decor.

Hal began browsing through the Gerard book, murmuring softly to himself. "'These herbs when they are green have the virtue to cool the hot burning of the liver.' Now isn't that a marvelous thing. I have chicory growing all over my place. I must give it a try."

"You can borrow the book if you like, Hal," Sage offered, "but I'll need it back soon."

"You are the soul of generosity," he said with a bow. "I'll have it back by Monday."

"While you're here, I'll return your copy of *The Sons of the Sheik*."

"How did you like it?"

"Not as good as *The Sheik*."

"You're right. It's a potboiler. I was disappointed in Hull. Still, it is a disgrace that *The Sheik* isn't in the standard reference books on literature. It had a vast influence on popular culture in the twenties." He took the two books and caressed them with the tenderness of a lover. "Did May say something about herbal tea?"

They returned to the patio. Wilf had small hope for the herbal tea. He considered it a beverage for invalids and the elderly, but he found its gentle taste soothing. When Hal took his leave later, May discreetly went inside to leave the young couple alone. "Since you did the cooking, Sage, I'll stack the dishes and tidy the kitchen," she said.

The moon had come out. It hung low in the sky, gleaming palely on the fields and casting an aura of romance on the setting.

"You don't really want to go for a drive, do you?" Sage asked, as he had mentioned it on the phone.

"I doubt we'd find anywhere prettier than this," he said. A feeling of contentment stole over him as he gazed afar, breathing in the sweet-smelling air. It was certainly better than city smog. His apartment in the city had a fine view, but it was a manmade view of buildings and lights and busy traffic below. This was more peaceful. Almost a sacred kind of peace. It reminded him in some vague way of being in church.

"I'll be converting you to a country mouse, at this rate," she said.

Their chairs sat side by side. Wilf reached out and grabbed her hand. "Is that why you invited me here?"

"No! I'm not trying to change you. I guess I just wanted you to know I don't live in a cultural or intellectual wasteland, like Hal said."

"I feel like a chump," he admitted. "That was damned condescending of me. I believe I called you a hippie, or something of the sort. Why didn't you tell me about your business background?"

"I intended to, but when you made that crack about the work ethic, I saw red. I work darned hard."

"Why'd you give up your job as a business consultant? I would have thought there'd be a great future there."

"So they told me. If money's all you're interested in, there was certainly a good future. I decided I wanted more. I wanted my life back. I wanted time for me." She turned and gazed at him with a lazy smile. "You should try it, Wilf."

"I take time for me," he said simply.

"How long since you've had a holiday?"

"Six months. I went skiing in Switzerland last winter. I was thinking of building a ski resort in Canada at the time. I thought I might get some ideas."

"That sounds like a busman's holiday," she said skeptically.

"I skied every day!" And had come home exhausted. He hadn't felt this relaxed and contented for as long as he could remember. "Maybe what I need is five acres in the country, like Hal," he said pensively.

"I might let you have five acres," she said, joking.

"How about letting me have a hundred and thirty-five?" he asked, half joking, but also curious to get her reaction. "It just occurred to me, you could keep your operation and still sell me enough land to build my golf course, along with Newton's farm."

She pouted. "I plan to expand. Besides, I don't want golf balls sailing through my windows, and hitting my workers as they cut the herbs."

"The course could be laid out in such a way that flying balls wouldn't be a problem."

Sage realized he was serious, and resented it. "No way," she said crossly. "There'd be tons of traffic and people."

"All potential customers for your shop."

"And look at all the heavy machinery and whatnot needed to lay out the course."

"All right. Don't have a fit," he said, squeezing her fingers placatingly. "It was just an idea."

Sage drew her hand away. She rose and walked to the railing to get rid of her pent-up anger. Her silken skirt whispered enticingly as she moved. Wilf rose and joined her.

"I still say you wouldn't get so angry if you weren't tempted," he said.

"It's not that." But of course she couldn't say what was really bothering her. She thought that once Wilf realized there was more to her than what appeared to be a flower child running a little herb shop, he'd take her seriously. He'd maybe admire her a little, and— But it was stupid to think about falling in love. She hardly knew him. It was just that he was the kind of man she *could* fall in love with, if he'd ever stop thinking about business.

She had put a lot of time and effort into this night, and this was what it came to in the end. He was still only interested in buying her farm. There was such a thing as the law of diminishing returns, and Sage felt she was investing her effort to no avail here.

"Well, it's getting late," she said, gazing at him wistfully. Yes, she could really have become very serious about this man. A sense of authority exuded from his proud, dark head and broad shoulders. Even in her angry mood, she felt the attraction to his masculinity. She wanted to cup his face in her two hands and savor the feel of his square jaw. She wanted to feel the fire of his lips again. Idiot! She tossed her head angrily, as if to cast off the spell.

Wilf watched her intently, trying to read her mood. "I think that's my cue to thank you for a lovely evening," he said in a querying voice. She just looked at him. "It was lovely, Sage. I had a very good time. Thank you."

"It was my pleasure."

He detected the edge of anger in her reply, and was sorry he'd spoiled the atmosphere. He never could forget business. Sage was right about that. She was a very special woman, and he hoped to follow up the acquaintance, whatever the outcome of buying her farm. But he sensed that this wasn't the moment to take her in his arms, as he wanted to.

Every item of the setting was perfect for it—the moonlight playing on her lovely face, the privacy. And he had blown it. "I'll call you before I leave town," he said.

"All right. Good night, Wilf."

A smile crinkled the corners of his eyes. In a mischievous mood, he said, "Good night, Gracie," and kissed the corner of her lips.

She smiled ruefully as his car left the farm. She liked a man with a sense of humor. Too bad business kept getting in the way. She went back into the kitchen and helped May clean up.

Chapter Five

When Wilf returned to his room at the Belview, he felt restless and dissatisfied. Work was his usual opiate, and he opened his briefcase to review his research on the Sanville golf course project. But he couldn't concentrate on business tonight. His mind kept drifting back to Sage on that patio with the sweet breeze lifting her hair. He wished he were still there, with her.

She'd be in his arms by now, if he hadn't botched it by letting talk of business intrude. His besetting sin. His last vacation had worn him out, trying to find time for a little skiing between work meetings. That compulsive streak was a carryover of his early days, when he was determined to make it—make it big.

But how big was big enough? He already had enough money that he could retire this very day and not have to worry. He had let work take over his life, and become an end in itself. Maybe it was time to relax a little and enjoy the fruits of his labor.

Sage wasn't interested in selling, so he'd just have to write her farm off and look elsewhere, but that didn't mean he had to write Sage off. A pity about the farm, though, because it really was an ideal location. Why couldn't she be reasonable? He'd settle for one hundred acres. Fifty acres was more than enough for her herb farm, since she'd taken up writing, as well. She only had fifteen acres under cultivation. She'd never expand to more than fifty in her lifetime, considering the labor-intensive nature of the product. Herbs were a relatively new crop in America. There was no machinery available for their harvesting, as far as he knew.

While the actual building of the golf course might be some inconvenience to Sage, once it was operating, she'd never know it was there. It seemed a shame to give up when all that was preventing the development and their mutual profit was her obstinacy.

Dammit, if she was such a hotshot businesswoman, she must see the advantage of his offer. And if she didn't, it was up to him to make her see it, because it was as much to her advantage as his. He'd sleep on it, and try to come up with something.

The problem didn't keep Wilf awake for long. He made it a rule not to take his business worries to bed with him. His mind was always clearer in the morning. After a bout of insomnia early in his career, he had learned relaxation exercises that were better than sleeping pills.

When his phone buzzed early the next morning, he was thankful for a good night's rest because Ken Carson had dumped a new problem in his lap.

"I found the site for our new golf course, Wilf," he announced, at seven-thirty in the morning. "You'll never guess what! Your secretary's uncle has a farm he's willing to sell."

Wilf's secretary, Anne Fine, had an uncle who'd been trying to unload his farm for as long as Wilf had known her. It consisted of a couple of hundred stony acres in the middle of nowhere. All it was good for was a quarry, and since it had already been excavated, it wasn't much good for anything except the birds and rabbits. The property was the wrong location, the wrong size, the wrong terrain.

"I've made a tentative offer. I'll be signing the deal today. Just thought I should let you know," Ken said proudly.

Wilf drew a deep sigh, but explaining was too much to contemplate so early in the morning. "Don't sign. I'll be there as soon as I can."

Wilf took a quick shave and shower, hurried into his clothes, grabbed a cup of coffee, and was on his way by eight. It was too early to phone Sage. He'd call her after he reached Buffalo.

His secretary was in the office and met him with a guilty smile. Anne Fine had worked for him for five years, and did more than type his letters. She was privy to all the details of his business transactions. She was a no-nonsense woman of forty, who looked a stylish thirty-five. She wore her copper hair in a sleek style and dressed in chic business suits.

"Ken told you," she said.

"Why did you let him do it?" he demanded.

"Wilf, it wasn't my fault. Ken did it on his own. Uncle Jack met me after work, and while I was powdering my nose, he convinced Ken his old farm was just what was needed."

Ken came out of his office when he heard Wilf's voice. "You want to be here for the signing," he said, smiling from ear to ear. "I'm really getting the knack of this real estate business, Wilf. I got him to sign an option for only five thousand bucks."

Wilf groaned.

"Sometimes I think Uncle Jack lives on all the options he's sold on those barren acres," Anne exclaimed. "So, what are we going to do?"

Wilf threw up his hands. "Let him keep the five thousand. It's cheaper than hiring lawyers to rescind the offer. You can tell him the deal's off, Anne. If we let Ken do it, we'll end up owning stony acres."

"It's a bargain!" Ken assured him. "He's only asking fifty thousand for it. It has a natural water hole and hilly terrain, just like you want."

Wilf patiently explained that the land was useless, and repeated that in the future Ken shouldn't sign anything without consulting him.

"Not even my credit cards?" Ken asked.

"You can buy gas and pay for restaurant meals on your personal cards, but don't use the company card," Anne said. "We didn't tell you the other bad news, Wilf. Ken bought himself a computer over the weekend. It's not compatible with our office system."

"It's got all kinds of games, though." Ken smiled.

Anne and Wilf exchanged a helpless shrug. "How'd it go at Sanville?" she asked.

"Sage won't sell. I'm thinking of making her an offer on a hundred acres, while she keeps fifty for her own operation. I hope she might go for that. I'll offer her the same price as I offered for the whole farm."

Anne whistled. "She'd be a fool if she didn't take it."

"That's what I thought. And the lady's no fool. In fact, she used to work as a business consultant, which means she's probably a damned sight smarter than we've been giving her credit for."

"Who'd she work for?" Anne asked.

Wilf wrinkled his brow, trying to remember. "I don't think she said. What difference does it make, anyway? She knows a lot about business. It was some city firm."

"Some of the local firms are pretty sleazy," Anne said. "I'll make a few calls and see if I can find out."

Wilf wasn't much interested. He went into his office to look over his agenda. It was there, half an hour later, that Anne found him.

"She worked for Mike Baxter," she announced with a meaningful look.

"Mike Baxter?" Wilf exclaimed. "I find that hard to believe."

"Believe it. And she left under rather peculiar circumstances."

"What do you mean?"

"She just upped and left. Used her holidays as notification time. She must have left them short-handed. She sounds pretty unreliable. But then, what can you expect of a Baxter employee? Mike Baxter's deals may be within the letter of the law, but he could show Machiavelli a few things."

"Where'd you hear this?" Wilf asked.

"From a friend who has a friend who was with Baxter at the time. Practically the horse's mouth. I bet your Sage Cramer's just been playing hard to get to raise her price," Anne said. "Baxter's consultants know all the tricks, and then some. The rumor was that they weren't above using romance with their clients to swing a deal."

"I'm sure Sage wouldn't do that," Wilf said stiffly.

Anne gave him a knowing grin. "I see she's got you conned. She must be good."

"You might as well phone your Uncle Jack now," he said curtly, and drew a letter forward to let Anne know the discussion was over.

He was just reaching for the phone to call Sage, but he drew his hand back. There couldn't be anything in what Anne had said...could there? Sage certainly hadn't discouraged his interest in her. In fact, she'd gone to a lot of trouble to excite his interest last night. Seeing that he didn't go for her country style, she'd switched to a smoother strategy.

A frown grew on Wilf's swarthy face as this idea took hold. He despised her tactics, but he had to admire her execution of them. She had really pulled out all the stops—the glamorous, come-hither dress to pique his desire, and the chaperon there to see he didn't get out of line. Even a college professor as a guest, to set the seal on her eminent respectability.

It nagged at his pride that he'd fallen for such an age-old stunt, like some rube who'd never met a beautiful woman before. She must have been laughing herself blue at him.

If she was using her beauty and charm as a lure, all he'd been allowed to do so far was look. Of course, men were always more eager before a conquest. Just how far would she be willing to go to get her price?

If Sage wanted to play in the deep end, he felt that he could match her for wits. He looked forward to the next step in the negotiations. In fact, he felt more comfortable playing with someone in his own league. Not that he stooped to such stunts himself, but it wasn't the first time he'd come across them. He didn't have to worry now that he was taking advantage of his colleague's innocence. It was time to turn up the heat.

His hand went out for the phone, but he drew it back. What was he doing? Sage wasn't like that. He'd let Anne's rumors and his own suspicious nature sway his instinctive feeling. He couldn't be that wrong about Sage.

He made his call, but May said she was out. "I told her I'd call before leaving Sanville," he said.

"She'll be sorry she missed you," May said.

"Tell her I called, will you?"

"I sure will."

In a way, he was grateful for the cooling-off period. It allowed him time to think things over. His feelings vacillated between disgust with Sage, and with himself for believing she was trying to dupe him. He thought she might return his call, but when she hadn't after two days, he decided he had to find out why, because the uncertainty was playing havoc with his concentration.

He wanted to see her again. Studying her in light of Anne's suspicions, he might see something in her that he'd missed before.

Ken came into his office that afternoon and lounged on the sofa. "I've decided to go to my cottage this weekend, Wilf. I don't suppose you'd like to come?" he asked hopefully.

"I thought I might go to Sanville," he said.

"Going to make another try for Sage's farm, are you?"

Wilf didn't answer. Let Ken think that was the reason.

"Very wise. You've given her a couple of days to stew, and fear she's lost the deal. But why not invite her to my place?" Ken suggested. "You can do your business there just as well."

Wilf looked interested. Sage would love Ken's place. It was a summer mansion on the eastern side of Lake Ontario. That would be a possible commute for Sage in her van. Where he saw her didn't really matter.

"I'll put on a real splash," Ken tempted. "Feel I owe you, after my five thousand dollar fiasco with Jack Fine. I've decided to pay for the computer out of my own pocket. Anne says since I use it mainly for playing computer games, we can't deduct it as an office expense."

"When are you going?" Wilf asked.

"This weekend coming up."

"Sage could be there before noon Saturday, if she's interested, that is."

"She'll be interested all right. You'll have Saturday afternoon and evening to explain the advantages of selling. Before she leaves on Sunday, she will have reconsidered, and be ready to sell. You won't get her land at any bargain basement price, but that's all right. I know you don't want to take advantage of her, which is more than she could say about you."

Wilf was hardly listening. No one paid much attention to Ken's ramblings. His own plans for the weekend were much more subtle. He just wanted to see Sage again, to talk to her. Of course, if she was interested in selling, if she'd been leading him on... Well, at least he'd end up with her farm.

"I'll ask Anne to take care of the party," Ken said, and buzzed for her to come into Wilf's office.

"We're having a party at my cottage this weekend," he said. "Wilf's inviting Sage Cramer to talk her into a deal."

"I'm **invit**ing her as a friend," Wilf said.

"Right, we won't spill the beans," Anne said knowingly.

"I'm serious, Anne."

"But you wouldn't say no if she seems agreeable?"

"Of course not."

"So, how big a party is it to be?" she asked.

Ken rubbed his ear and looked at Wilf. "It's your party," Wilf reminded him.

"Right. We'll keep the number of houseguests to a minimum, and have one big bash on Saturday night. Now, who shall we invite for the weekend?"

"Am I invited?" Anne asked. "It sounds like fun. Besides, I'm dying to get a look at this Cramer woman."

"Come along if you're willing to give up your weekend," Ken said.

"We'll want an older couple as chaperons," Wilf said.

Anne laughed. "Chaperons! What is this Sage Cramer? A nun?"

Wilf didn't deign to answer that gibe. "I'll invite her Aunt May and her professor friend, Hal Jenkins, if that's all right with you, Ken?"

"Fine, the more the merrier," Ken agreed.

"So we set up one big party on Saturday night. The sort of party that would impress even an ex-employee of Baxter's," Anne said. She avoided looking at Wilf as she said that. "I'll invite some of our clients, and Ken can give me a list of the local worthies. You play golf there, Ken. You must know some people."

"I must, if I could only think of their names. I'll check my black book."

He went back to his office and Wilf gave Anne a pointed look. "This isn't what you think, Anne. I'm not trying to con a client," he said.

"You never con your clients! I'm sure you plan to make a generous offer. But let's not lose sight of one point. Maybe the potential client is trying to con us. They say you can't con a con man."

Wilf frowned at this reminder of the situation. "If she does want to sell, there's no harm done," he said. "And if she doesn't want to, she won't. She's had a nice weekend holiday."

Ken returned and handed Anne an address book. "You might find some names in there. I draw a little golf club if they're golfing buddies, and the initial tells you where they're from. The ones from my cottage area have a *W,* for Westport. You can invite any of the *W*'s. I'll be glad to get some use out of the cottage. I'll get right on to Mrs. Esmond. That's my housekeeper."

When he left, Anne said to Wilf, "I'd better see that he does it. With that new computer to amuse him, he might forget all about it. Have you called Sage yet?"

"No, I'll wait until tomorrow, to see that you and Ken get this party together. I hate having to rescind an invitation."

Anne followed Ken to his office, where he was searching his Rolodex for the phone number of his cottage. "I feel this woman is taking advantage of Wilf," she said.

"No, she's all right. She's very pretty."

"I know she's pretty, Ken. That's just the trouble. Wilf's obviously bowled over by her. He's never let a woman interfere with business before. He's inviting chaperons to this party, for crying out loud. I plan to sound Miss Cramer out and see for myself that she's on the level, since you two can't see past her pretty face."

"Wilf won't want you interfering."

"I know. That's why we're not going to tell him."

"Tell him what?"

"That we're sounding out Sage Cramer. I have a pretty good eye for judging people. I'll soon know if she's on the up and up."

"She won't let anything slip if she knows you're Wilf's secretary. She's pretty, but she's smart."

"Damn, that's right. We won't tell her."

"Maybe Wilf will let it slip. I mean, over a whole weekend, it's bound to come out. He'd never go along with lying about it."

"I wouldn't dare ask him to. He says he doesn't plan to talk business, so it might not come up. We'll create a different impression."

"Like what?" Ken asked in confusion.

"Like that you and I are lovers," she said. "If Sage gets that idea in her head, she won't look any further for why I'm there."

"But you're not my type!" Ken said, horrified.

"And you are not mine, I assure you. It's called acting."

"That's sneaky!" Ken exclaimed.

"Only if she's being sneaky. If she's on the up and up, there's no harm done. We have to look out for the firm's interests, Ken. You cost us five thousand this week."

"I said I'd pay it myself."

"You know Wilf won't let you. The least you can do is prevent Wilf from throwing away more money."

"Then why do I feel sneaky about helping you?"

"That's your sensitive conscience," she told him.

"Right. My dad told me the first thing you have to get rid of in business is your conscience."

"And you have to be subtle," Anne added. "We won't tell Wilf about our little plan. I'll just quietly talk to Miss Cramer, sometime when we're alone, and find out what she's really like. You can leave it all up to me."

"Right. You'll handle it. Now, what was I supposed to do?"

"You phone your housekeeper and tell her to prepare the cottage for Saturday."

"Right—I'm having a party."

"And I'm having a few reservations about my plan," Anne admitted. "But it's for Wilf's and the company's good. We don't want some pretty hussy putting a fast one over on him. He always played straight with his clients, and we have to see that he isn't taken advantage of."

In his office, Wilf was more troubled by the idea Anne had planted in his mind than he liked to admit. Was Sage trying to con him? There was an innocence to her at times that made the idea laughable. And if she was perfectly innocent, he'd feel like a heel, with everyone scheming behind her back. He had a pretty good idea why Anne Fine had invited herself to this party. She was up to something. And then there was that other more worldly side to Sage. She was two or three women in one.

A glazed look came into his eyes as he remembered her long blond hair, flowing in the wind, and her dreamy green eyes. That was the flower child. But she was also a sultry siren, and possibly an exceptionally shrewd businesswoman, since she'd worked for Mike Baxter. Why had she concealed that?

* * *

At home, Sage continued with her usual chores. She found herself spending more time in the house than she should after missing Wilf's call, waiting in vain for the phone to ring again. It was funny he didn't call back. In the evening she and May drove into Sanville to a movie, because Sage knew she wouldn't be able to work, and the night would seem endless.

He called that evening at ten-thirty, after she returned from the movie. "Sage, I've been trying to get you all evening," he said.

"Oh, May and I were out. Where are you?"

"I'm in Buffalo." Sage felt the rising excitement dwindle. "I wanted to thank you for that lovely dinner. It was marvelous. Something came up at the office and I had to leave Sanville too early to call you before I left. I didn't want you to think I'd forgotten you."

"I understand," she said softly. "I don't suppose you'll be back this way soon?"

"It's hard to say, but if I am, may I call you?"

"Yes, I'd like that."

They chatted for a few moments, then hung up. Wilf didn't plan to mention the visit to Ken's cottage until it was all firmed up. Her wistful remarks had told him that she was interested in him. A voice at the back of his mind prodded, "Or she wants you to think she is."

Sage was glad he'd called again, but as far as she was concerned, that seemed like the end of it. She doubted she'd ever see Wilf Jameson again. He'd probably be building a shopping mall in Texas, or a marina in Florida, or a condo in New York. Too bad it hadn't worked out. Since she knew she'd have trouble sleeping, she brewed a pot of chamomile tea and began researching her next column.

She decided to do lemon balm. Its botanical name was *Melissa officinalis,* which was the Greek translation for bee. In the old days, monks used it to attract bees, and to make lemon balm honey. The herb was associated with love. Lovers long ago used to wear arm bands of it, to secure happiness in their love. Of course, she'd include more practical information, too, like its cultivation and multi-purposes. It was good in a potpourri and cooking. She'd submit some recipes such as lemon balm sauce for fish, and stuffing for fowl.

As she jotted down her notes, she kept harking back to the herb's association with love. Maybe if she'd served Wilf lemon balm tea instead of chamomile... Such nonsense! That sort of conjuring, while interesting, was mere folklore. She'd just have to forget Wilf Jameson.

The next day Sage got her largest order yet, from a health-food chain in California. Between exhilaration and the busyness of this particular season, she managed to move Wilf to the back of her mind the next day, if she couldn't quite forget him. Really they weren't well suited at all. His personality and modus operandi comprised everything she had decided she wanted to escape from. A high-tension life-style, overwork, a zealously sharp focus on the profit motive. These were not bad things, necessarily, but not what she wanted.

May was having a few friends in for cards that evening, which left Sage free to write her column. She was at her word processor at nine o'clock when the phone rang. She let May take it on the house phone, as most of the calls were for her.

In a minute, May's head appeared at the door. "It's for you, Sage. Sounds like Wilf."

"Wilf!" May noticed the smile of surprise.

"Maybe you should let him have a few acres," May said, and laughed as she closed the door.

"Sage, it's Wilf Jameson here. Remember me?"

"Of course I remember you, Wilf. Where are you?" Please let him be in Sanville!

"In Buffalo."

Her eager smile faded. "Oh. Are you coming this way?" she asked, wondering why he was phoning.

"I wish I could, but business..."

"I hope this isn't another attempt to get me to sell my farm," she said, becoming annoyed at the thought. That's what it always was with Wilf. She'd let her hopes rise for nothing.

"I have something else in mind this time," he said. But he made note of what was at the forefront of her mind—her farm and his golf course. "Are you free this weekend?"

"What time on the weekend? Do you mean Saturday evening, or—"

"I meant the whole weekend, actually. My friend has a cottage on Lake Ontario. I thought we might spend Saturday and Sunday there."

She stared at the phone in disbelief. If Wilf had been there in person, she would have slapped him. "I'm afraid not," she said, very coldly.

"Not free, or not interested?"

"Not interested. Goodbye, Wilf."

"Wait! Don't hang up. This isn't what you think. I meant you and May—and Hal Jenkins, too, if he'd like to come. It's a small party. There'll be another woman and my business partner from the office. He owns the cottage actually." Wilf hoped the weekend hadn't sounded too much like a backyard boardroom retreat. That wasn't what it was, as far as he was concerned. Of course, he wouldn't refuse if she wanted to do some business.

"One of your working holidays," she said, her ire changing to curiosity.

"That seems to be the only kind I can manage, but I do plan to take in some leisure time. I'd like to spend it with you."

"Gee, I don't know, Wilf. I'm awfully busy," she said, but her instinct was to accept. "I must fill a really huge order from an outfit in California. It'll mean that I can get ten more acres into production sooner than I hoped," she explained.

Wilf frowned at that. This news could be advance notice that her price was rising by the day. The timing of this "really huge order" was suspicious to say the least.

"That's great, Sage," he said, trying to sound happy for her. "But couldn't you follow your own advice and take a few days off?"

Wilf's encouragement was all she needed to make up her mind. "You're right. I'm supposed to be enjoying life as well as working. I accept. When and where?"

He gave her instructions. She agreed to ask May and Hal and phone him back as soon as possible. As Hal was playing cards with May just outside the door, it didn't take five minutes.

In fact, Wilf timed it, and was a little surprised at her eagerness. In four minutes and thirty seconds his phone rang. He expected he'd have to wait until morning.

"Hi, it's me," Sage said breathlessly. "It's all set."

"How'd you manage it so quickly? You've hardly had time to call Hal."

"Not necessary. He was here. We'll arrive Saturday morning around eleven. Since it's a cottage, I assume casual clothes are all we'll need?"

"I believe Ken—that's my partner—plans to have friends over on Saturday evening. He mentioned a party—not a barbecue-type party. Dinner, dancing. Better bring one dress. May I suggest that creation you wore to your own party?"

"Did you like it?" she asked.

Her tone was shyly pleased. "It was a knockout. Or maybe it was the woman who was wearing it," he added in a husky voice.

Emboldened by his tone, she said flirtatiously, "Why don't I wear something else, and we'll see whether it was the dress or the model."

"You do that. I have a feeling that the dress wasn't the main attraction."

"I'll see you Saturday morning, then. I'm looking forward to it, Wilf."

"So am I."

It was the proper moment to say goodbye and hang up. Strangely, Wilf felt a reluctance to do so. "What are you doing?" he asked. "Since Hal is there, I thought maybe I was interrupting a discussion on rare books, or something."

"No, he's just playing cards with my aunt and some friends. I'm in my office, working on next week's column."

An image of her office rose in his mind, with the word processor and computer and Sage in that wonderful gauzy dress. "What's next week's subject?" he asked, to prolong the conversation.

"Lemon balm. You've probably never heard of it."

"I've heard of lemon, and I've heard of balm, but not together, and not as a plant. What is it?"

"It's a perennial herb that grows to a foot or two high, light green leaves, light mauve flowers, not terribly attractive. Easy to grow, but it'll take over if you don't cut it back."

"It sounds predatory, like crabgrass. Why waste a column on it?"

"Oh no! It's romantic." Her voice softened to intimacy. "It's associated with lovers."

"Ah, well in that case, I approve."

After an awkward little silence, she asked, "What are you doing, Wilf?"

"Thinking about lemon balm, and you, and lovers. I'd better let you get back to work, before you lose your train of thought." Sage felt she had already done that. For the rest of the evening, her mind would be full of Wilf, and the weekend.

"Yes, I'd better say goodbye."

"I'm a little surprised to hear that a dedicated relaxer like you is working so late. You're not taking your own advice."

"Advice is easier to give than to take, isn't it?" She laughed.

"You're right, but I'm going to take your advice anyway, and stop work now. See you Saturday. Good night, Sage."

"Good night."

She hung up, and sat smiling at her word processor. There were dozens of plans she should be making. She'd have to arrange for someone to oversee the work on Saturday, and make out a timetable for the shop, and plan something to wear. But tomorrow was soon enough. For now she'd just take her own advice and relax, enjoy the anticipation of this little holiday.

It seemed Wilf was interested in her as a woman, not just a potential client. Since that was the case, she could admit to herself what she already knew anyway, deep down inside. She was falling in love with him, if she wasn't quite in love yet. Sure, he was a little more persistent than she'd liked about buying her farm, but that was his aggressive business side at work. She understood that compulsive streak. Most successful entrepreneurs had it. There was another side, too. The side that had raved over her blue dress...

She helped May make tea and served some food to the cardplayers when their game was finished. While doing it, she mentioned to Hal and May that they should take one party outfit with them on Saturday.

"Wilf Jameson, eh?" Hal said musingly. "He seemed like a nice fellow. I wonder if there's a golf course near this cottage. I'll take along my clubs, just in case."

"And I'll get my hair done before we go," May said.

Sage wouldn't bother getting her hair done. Since there'd probably be boating and swimming to contend with, she planned to wear her hair up. Her main concerns were arranging for help at the farm while she was away.

Her most trusted employee was only twenty-one years old, but he was a third-year agriculture student. Percy Henson knew more about her plants than she did herself. He was completely trustworthy, and he was always happy to get extra hours as he was financing his education.

All the business arrangements were made by Friday afternoon. In the evening, Sage turned her thoughts to packing. She wanted to wear something special for the party on Saturday evening. Wilf had really liked her blue silky dress, which was floating and romantic.

She examined her dresses carefully, and finally made her choice. With one of her bonuses from Baxter and Associates she had splurged and bought a French couture cocktail gown. The dress was made with spaghetti straps and came to mid-calf. The mint-green chiffon material shimmered like water when she moved. It clung to her breasts and small waist, and billowed like sea foam below. Maybe a bit fancy for a cottage party, but she had a feeling Wilf's friends would be from the upper echelon of business, and she wanted him to be proud of her.

It was sweet of him to have included May and Hal in the invitation. It assured her that he appreciated her scruples about spending a weekend alone with a man. She didn't have to worry that things would get out of control. She went to bed early, to be well rested for the drive, and the two days ahead.

Chapter Six

Hal phoned early on Saturday to tell Sage he was going to take his own car, in case he wanted to go off in search of a golf course. Sage had already decided to leave Percy the van and drive her Porsche. She dressed in comfortable tan culottes and a cotton shirt for the drive, and wore a straw hat to keep the sun from slanting in above her sunglasses.

"Dull," May called the outfit. Her own sundress, a riot of gaudy flowers, certainly added vivid color to the couple.

They headed out at nine-thirty for the drive to Westport, where Ken Carson's cottage was located.

It was a bright summer morning, the type of morning that made you glad you were alive. A few innocent white puffball clouds loitered in the azure sky. A drift of crown vetch blanketed the banks of the highway in pink blossoms. In the distance, wildflowers spotted the meadows, but for Sage, it was anticipation of the weekend ahead with Wilf that added a special fillip to the trip.

She enjoyed giving her Porsche a good workout. The only difficulty was restraining it to the speed limit. It seemed to accumulate the miles as though the speedometer was set to warp speed, and cornered so neatly that Sage decided she should drive it more often.

At the little village of Westport she stopped to check the map. Carson's cottage was called Shangri-la, but Sage certainly didn't expect anything in the way of a Tibetan monastery. The cottages in the area all had fanciful names. She had passed signs announcing Valhalla and Paradise Regained.

A mile out of Westport, a fingerboard sign pointed to Shangri-la, and she turned into an unpaved, twisty lane, where branches reached out and brushed her car.

"If we meet anyone on this track, one of us will have to back up. There isn't room for two jackrabbits to pass," May complained.

"I'm afraid I'll break my muffler," Sage said as she bumped over a pothole.

"I hope the cottage has indoor plumbing," May said doubtfully.

"I'm sure it has," Sage replied, but she was beginning to think her Paris original might be overkill.

The twisty lane continued for a quarter of a mile. Then it turned a corner, and before them lay a veritable mansion. Stone walls spread along a curve of the river. A slate roof, white columns, and double oak doors gave the "cottage" the air of a municipal building in some large city.

"Good Lord! This can't be it!" May exclaimed.

"It's the only house we've passed," Sage said, but she felt a twinge of doubt, too.

An oversize collie ran out to meet them. "It's a good thing I didn't bring Whiskers," May said. "I just hope Percy remembers to feed him."

The dog's barking soon alerted the others, and the front door opened. Wilf stepped out, waving. His eyes widened slightly at the Porsche. Sage hadn't driven that in Sanville!

Sage pulled into the circular drive and got out. Wilf came hurrying forward to meet her. There was a self-conscious moment while they stood, smiling at each other, each wondering if they should exchange a greeting kiss.

Wilf looked so happy to see her that Sage decided a kiss was appropriate. She rose on tiptoe and placed a little kiss at the edge of his lips.

"Hi, Wilf. It's nice to see you again."

He placed his hands on her arms and squeezed lightly as he returned the greeting. Her warm smile and the sparkle in her eyes told him Sage considered this visit a date. A woman didn't look like that when she was thinking of business. He'd been a fool to let Anne undermine his faith in Sage.

"Hi, Wilf. Where do we park?" May called from the car.

He accompanied Sage to the car and slid into the front seat, displacing poor May to straddling the center console. "I'll show you. The garage is just around to your left. Don't worry about luggage. It'll be taken up to your rooms."

As Sage drove on, May said, "I guess we don't have to worry about indoor plumbing. We had a few doubts as we came along that bumpy road. That mausoleum is big enough for an indoor golf course."

In the garage, four of the six parking spaces were already filled. Along with Wilf's car, there was another expensive sports car, a van, and an ordinary compact car.

"What, no Rolls-Royce?" May joked.

"That's probably warehoused at his town house," Sage said, shaking her head at some people's idea of a cottage. Having worked with some of Baxter's wealthy clients, she wasn't as bowled over as May, but she was impressed.

She parked the car, and as they returned to the house, Sage had time for a more leisurely examination of Wilf. He was wearing a pale blue polo shirt, light tan jeans and sneakers, and still managed to look both sexy and elegant. His broad shoulders filled the shirt without straining it. His jeans clung to long legs and a board-flat stomach. Sage was sorry he was wearing sunglasses that robbed her of a good look at his face. His smile was certainly warm, but she wanted to see his eyes. She had a feeling her own eyes betrayed too much pleasure at seeing him.

"What a shack! This friend of yours must be a millionaire," May said, shaking her head.

"He doesn't have to worry about making his car payments," Wilf agreed. "Shall we go inside and meet our host?"

"I'm dying to see the inside," May said, and they all went in.

A white and black parquet-look marble floor seemed a bit much, even to Wilf. He was careful not to point out the overhead chandelier.

"Is this supposed to be a cottage?" May asked, looking around at the formal entrance, where a huge urn containing a big bouquet of freshly cut flowers rested on a half table beneath an ornate mirror.

"It was built for a beer baron at the turn of the century," Wilf explained. "These places were going at bargain prices after the war, when Ken's dad picked it up."

He led them along a hallway to the rear of the house, and out a door to a sweep of veranda overlooking the river. The St. Lawrence was so wide that Canada was just a green blur on the other side. A cooling breeze stirred the trees that bordered the shining water.

Sage hadn't spared much thought to the owner of Shangri-la. She expected he'd be a reincarnation of some millionaire from days past, probably wearing a navy blazer and ascot. But the man Wilf was leading her to looked like an overgrown kid. A close-fitting T-shirt wasn't the optimum outfit for his protruding tummy. Neither were his shorts of a brilliant red and blue plaid. She looked at Ken Carson, blinked, and frowned. She'd seen that little man before. Where was it?

Ken stepped forward with his hand out. "Ken Carson. Remember me, Ms. Cramer?"

"Oh, yes, at the herb farm!" she exclaimed, suddenly recollecting. "Please call me Sage. This is my aunt, May Cramer."

"And this is my friend, Mrs. Fine," Ken said. A piercing look from Anne reminded him of his role. "A very special friend," he added.

Anne came forward to shake the new guests' hands. "Don't be so formal, Ken. Call me Anne, please," she added, smiling at the new arrivals.

They exchanged a quick perusal of each other. As there was no Mr. Fine present, Sage quickly pegged Anne as a rich widow. Her simply styled sundress probably carried a designer label. To judge by her sleek hairdo and carefully manicured nails, she spent a lot of time at the beauty parlor. She looked a little old for Ken, but their manner indicated they were indeed special friends.

Anne withheld her conclusion on Sage. She was a beauty, all right. Easy to see how Wilf had fallen for her. He hadn't taken his eyes off her since they came in, and he was smiling like an idiot. Everyone shook hands. When the introductions were finished, Ken said, "What can we get you folks to drink?"

"A beer would hit the spot," May said, sinking into a deeply upholstered lounge chair under an umbrella.

After a quick glance to see what the others were having, Sage opted for a Bloody Mary. They settled around the umbrella-shaded table to become acquainted.

Compliments to Ken were the first item to be disposed of.

"I hardly ever use the cottage. It's too big," Ken said dismissively. "I keep trying to get Wilf to turn it into a summer hotel."

"I did a feasibility study," Wilf explained. "It's inconveniently large for a private house, but not big enough to make a profitable hotel. It only has nine bedrooms."

"Only nine," May said, biting back a grin.

Wilf continued. "The land's certainly worth something, but it seems a shame to destroy a lovely old house like this."

"Oh, you mustn't!" Sage exclaimed. "They don't build houses like this anymore."

"A white elephant," Ken grumbled. "I'm hoping to unload it on a company that's looking for a conference center. Of course, it'd mean a new road. The road into this place is a disgrace."

"We noticed," May agreed.

"I keep telling him to get it repaired," Anne said.

"I had to buy a little van to use while I'm here," Ken complained. "The chassis's high off the road. I'm afraid of wrecking my car."

Since he only came here occasionally, Sage wondered why he'd "had" to buy a van. Money was obviously no object to Ken. She was curious about why he had been at her farm, and asked him.

"I work with Wilf," he explained. "He asked me to have a look at your place for him."

"I see." This must be the rich cousin Wilf had mentioned.

"But don't worry that we mean to plague you about selling this weekend," Ken added.

Wilf felt uncomfortable with this subject. He flickered a glance at Sage to catch her reaction. So far as he could tell, she wasn't particularly interested. Relief was as close as he could come to judging her reaction.

"I'm sure you'll find the perfect location," she said.

There was a moment's uncomfortable silence, then Ken said, "Actually I took an option on another farm."

"Oh really? Which one?" Sage asked, thinking it must be one of her neighbors.

"It isn't near Sanville," Wilf said. "Actually it isn't suitable."

When Wilf went to the drinks table, Anne rose nonchalantly and followed him. "Sage is very pretty," she said. She gave him a cagey look. "I noticed she drives a Porsche. I saw it as she drove in. I wouldn't think a little herb farmer ran into that kind of money."

"She worked before she inherited the farm," he replied.

"Yes, we mustn't forget her working for Baxter," Anne said, splashing tomato juice into her glass. She leveled a meaningful look at Wilf, then returned to join the others.

When Wilf joined the party, he saw the subject of his projected golf course hadn't dropped, as he'd hoped.

"You lost out on a good deal, Sage," May said. "It'll take you years to make as much as Wilf offered you."

"Like Wilf said, the farm we have an option on isn't really suitable," Ken repeated Wilf's sternly delivered comment. "So it's not too late to change your mind." He stared expectantly at Sage.

Sage noticed Wilf's discomfort with the conversation. She had also noticed that little tête-à-tête with Anne Fine. What was going on there? Her eyes, when she looked at Wilf, were clouded with suspicion.

"What seems to be the problem with the farm you optioned, Wilf?" she asked.

"It isn't in exactly the location we favored and the spread isn't quite large enough."

"Where is it?" Sage asked.

"It's southwest of Buffalo."

That wouldn't attract exactly the clientele Wilf had been after, but Sage assumed he'd done his homework, and would never have optioned this new location if it weren't a good investment.

The slightly strained conversation was interrupted by the arrival of Hal Jenkins, and the talk turned to praise of Shangri-la once again. Hal had a drink and entertained them with the history of Shangri-la. "From James Hilton's novel, *Lost Horizon*," he said. "A magical place where people stay young as long as they remain at the monastery, and assume their proper age when they leave."

"Is that right!" Ken exclaimed. "I never knew that."

Sage just smiled at his lack of interest in never even bothering to investigate the name of his own property.

"Maybe I should keep it and retire here," he joked.

"You certainly wouldn't have any trouble renting those nine bedrooms if you've found the secret of perpetual youth, Ken," Anne said. "I'd gladly live here myself."

Sage examined her closely while she spoke, and decided Anne was a little older than she had first thought. Still attractive, though. She seemed more interested in Ken than he was in her.

At noon, a male servant in a short white jacket came and told them luncheon was served.

"Boy, you really know how to live, Ken," May congratulated him.

"Tommy's really my servant in town," Ken explained. "I only have a housekeeper here, Mrs. Esmond. When I have guests, I have to hire temporary help."

"Poor you," May said satirically. "When we have guests at the farm, we have to do all the work ourselves. Don't expect any sympathy from me for your servant problems."

Wilf escorted Sage into the dining room, where a formal table was laid. The cutlery had the aged patina of sterling silver. Prisms dancing on the linen cloth announced that the wineglasses were real crystal—at a cottage. And the floral centerpiece looked as if it had been professionally arranged. Such perfectly matched roses didn't usually grow in untended gardens.

Over soup, a delicate bouillon, Hal Jenkins gave a lecture on servants over the centuries, as seen in literature.

"Even what we would call relatively poor people today had a servant in the nineteenth century," he explained. "They might do without a carriage, but to be without a servant was unthinkable. A lady didn't do her own housework."

"Then I'm no lady," May said bluntly.

"All that changed, of course, with the industrial revolution," Hal continued, and followed the course of history as they ate their soup.

Over the main course of curried shrimp and rice he discussed golf. Wilf was beginning to regret he'd invited this talking machine. It was hard to get a word in edgewise. And when the subject did eventually change, he almost wished it hadn't.

Hal said, "So you won't be building your golf course at Sage's place, eh, Wilf? I'm sorry to hear it, in a way. We really need a good course."

"I haven't given up on the general area, if I could find the right location." He purposely didn't look at Sage, but he waited to hear if she would say anything.

"There's a big cattle farm about five miles from my place," she mentioned. "It has nice rolling countryside. I don't know whether they'd consider selling, but it might be worth a shot. I know the owner's getting on in years. I met him at a fall fair last year. The farm's called Helvetia, if you're interested in looking into it, Wilf. The owner's name is Steinem."

"Thanks for the tip. I might do that," he said. This tip confirmed that Sage had no interest whatsoever in selling her own farm. And that put Wilf in an embarrassing position, since Anne and Ken were convinced she was only trying to raise her price. In a way, he was misleading her, and that was a dirty trick to play on a nice woman.

He felt badly about that, yet he felt a bubble of joy beneath the shame. He was happy to know that Sage wasn't the schemer he had feared she was. If she was really what she seemed to be, she was one woman in a million. She had given up the very profitable rat race at Baxter's to follow her dream. It was a lot of risk and hard work. As May said, it would take her years to make as much as he'd offered, but she wouldn't give up her dream.

After lunch, Ken asked what everyone would like to do. "Anne and I are taking the launch out. Anne knows how to steer it," he admitted shamelessly. "I never got the hang of it myself."

"I'm for golf!" Hal announced. "Will you come with me, May? Your drives need practice."

"You want a caddie, you mean!" she retorted.

"Use my golf cart," Ken offered. "If you're planning to play at the Westport Golf Club, that is. I have one there. Never use it."

"I don't have any clubs," May said.

"I have a set of clubs there, too, in my locker. I'll phone the club and tell them you want to use them."

"There you are, then, no excuse," Hal exclaimed.

"I guess there's no way out," May said, and agreed.

"How about you and Wilf, Sage?" Ken asked.

Sage said, "I'd like to just roam through your fields for a bit, Ken, if that's all right. Maybe have a swim later."

"Sounds pretty dull." Ken frowned. "That's the trouble with cottages. Nothing to do. You end up going out in boats, or swimming, but this is the first time anyone's sunk to going for a walk. I ought to put in tennis courts."

"I'm always curious to see what wild herbs are around," Sage explained. "Maybe I'll harvest some seeds, if I find I don't have the plant. I found some wild yarrow at a friend's cottage last summer. Is it okay if I help myself to a few samples of your plants?"

"Feel free. Take whatever you want."

"Sounds like a working holiday to me," Wilf joked.

"Guilty, as charged. It's hard to stop, when your job is also your hobby."

"The best of all possible worlds." Hal smiled. "Go and *cultivez votre jardin*. Voltaire's *Candide*," he explained to his bewildered audience. "It is his recipe for happiness, to cultivate one's garden, either literally or metaphorically."

"It's not my idea of happiness." Ken frowned. "But there is a garden out back. Will you be wanting any tools, Sage?"

"No, thanks," she replied. "I always carry a little hand spade with me. You never know when you might find a treasure."

"You certainly won't be able to dig for treasure with a hand spade."

Anne rolled her eyes ceilingward. "Come along, Ken."

"Are you going with them?" Sage asked Wilf.

"No, with you, if you'll let me."

She smiled her pleasure. "I'd be happy for your company, but I hope you're not bored."

A special smile bloomed in his eyes and slowly traced its way down to his lips. "I don't think that'll be a problem," he said. "Where do you keep that spade?"

"In my purse." She drew out a small spade in a plastic jacket. Wilf shook his head in disbelief. She drew out another parcel. "This one has little envelopes for collecting seeds, and, of course, a pen to identify them."

"I see you take your herbs very seriously!"

"They're practically my life," she admitted. "That's why I could never think of selling my farm. I'm sorry I couldn't help you out there, but I could never sell Grandpa's farm."

"I understand," he said in a quiet voice.

Wilf had a sinking feeling that before the weekend was over, the whole truth would come out. And the whole truth was that he had half believed she wanted to sell her farm to him at her price. It would be better if she heard it from him.

He determined on the spot that he'd explain and apologize before this weekend was over. If he blurted out the truth now, he was afraid she'd leave, but after they came to know each other better, he'd tell her. He didn't want any secrets, because it was no longer Sage's property he wanted. He was very interested in her as a woman.

They went down to the dock to wave Anne and Ken off in the boat. It was a huge, sleek fiberglass inboard that would hold a dozen people. Ken sat with his arms crossed, looking bored to tears, and they hadn't even left the dock yet. When Anne started the motor, his head jerked back, and the boat shot forth, leaving a wake of foam behind.

"We have five acres to explore," Wilf said, taking Sage's hand and leading her into the meadow.

"Poor Ken doesn't seem to get much pleasure from all his money, does he?" she said.

"He has no idea how to manage either his life or his money. His father left him very well off, so he never had to work. He was frittering his life away, traveling and buying frivolous things, like that van that he never uses. I invited him to become a partner in my company. Mostly he provided capital, but I try to keep him busy and out of trouble, too. That's why he visited you, to take a look at your operation."

"And when he failed, you sent in the big gun—you," she said.

"That's about it. I'm sorry I pestered you about that, Sage. I just wasn't sure your no meant no."

"I understand. I certainly wouldn't have jumped up and down and yelled 'yippee' even if I had wanted to sell," she admitted.

"It's nice that you are a businesswoman yourself. You understand certain practices...." He waited. If she was encouraging, he'd confess on the spot and get it over with, because the idea kept nagging at him that Ken would blurt it all out in some offensive way before long.

"At least you're honest about it, Wilf." His heart shrank. Honest! He felt like a crook. "That's nothing to some of the stuff that went on at Baxter's. Once old Mike retired and his son took over, the integrity took a nosedive. Baxter's is the consulting firm I worked for. I didn't want to be associated with an outfit like that. Oh, they were very successful, but making money isn't everything. I left soon after young Mike's agenda became clear to me."

"That's why you left?" he asked.

"That's one of the reasons. If it hadn't been for the farm, I would just have joined some more reputable company. I've never regretted leaving the business. Oh, look! It's ginseng!" she exclaimed, rushing to bend over a little plant about a foot tall, with white flowers.

"Time to get out the spade?" he asked.

"Better not! It's been overcollected. It's a threatened species. I'll leave it, and hope it spreads. Digging this up would be like shoplifting. It doesn't belong to me, but to nature."

"What's it used for?" Wilf asked, but his mind wasn't really on the question. He was taking note that Sage's ethical code was so unshakable and so ingrained that she wouldn't even take an herb, which she obviously wanted. No one was watching; Ken had given his permission, but it was against her principles. The main reason he had ever doubted her integrity was that she'd worked for Baxter, and now that he knew why she'd left, he felt worse than ever.

"It's used as a tonic," she explained. "People make tea out of it. Some think it's an aphrodisiac," she said disparagingly. "I doubt there's any such thing. Who'd want the kind of love that had to be chemically, or in this case, herbally induced?"

They continued their stroll. By a stream, she identified watercress. "I don't have a stream on my property, or I'd gather some of this," she said. "It belongs to the nasturtium family, but this variety likes wet roots."

"I don't have to ask what watercress is for. It's for sandwiches at English tea parties."

"And for salads. I never thought it had much taste myself."

She found other treasures, and dug up some wild garlic and dill, but mostly they just strolled and talked. Wilf was impressed at her love of not only herbs but all of nature. She could identify wildflowers he'd seen all his life, but couldn't name.

"That's cinquefoil," she said, looking at a low-growing yellow flower. "It means five leaves, in French. The flower has five leaves, of course. And that tall, pointed flower by the stream is purple loosestrife—it's becoming a menace to our wetlands. I won't spread that, although it's very pretty. This is Queen Anne's lace," she said, fingering a tall plant with a flat white circle of small flowerets on top.

She picked one and handed it to Wilf. "See the one little colored flower in the center, sort of a blackish red? This acts as a lure to attract insects and get it pollinated. The insects think it's a fly or something, and come to investigate. Isn't nature clever?" She laughed.

"I had no idea old Mother Nature was such a con artist."

"Oh, sure she is. Look at all the harmless insects that can disguise themselves as more dangerous species for protection, and the ones that are just the opposite. They look harmless, but are really dangerous. They're as bad as people. Present company excluded, of course." With a sweet and trusting smile, she reached out and touched his hand. Wilf's fingers closed possessively over hers, and they continued their walk, hand in hand.

Sunlight dappled her face as they passed under a growth of small trees. This seemed the proper setting for Sage; not the fancy party Anne and Ken were planning. But he couldn't put all the blame on them. He had acquiesced, and that made him a partner in the deceit.

Sage was a nature girl, as unspoiled as that white flower she was holding. When she looked up at him, he felt the breath catch in his lungs. He wanted to gather her in his arms and kiss her, but he was afraid to.

He felt unworthy of her. He usually prided himself on his moral conduct, but he saw there were degrees of morality. He was not bad; Sage was good. By going along with Anne, he was acting like one of those predator insects who had masqueraded himself in innocence to lure her. Or at least, that was the way she'd see him when she learned the truth. He felt an overpowering urge to tell her everything, right then and there.

He stopped and took the flower from her. "Sage, about your farm," he said reluctantly.

He watched as her sweet smile faded, and another expression seized her face. Not anger; it wasn't that. It was worse. Her questioning look slowly turned to regret. "No, I'm not trying to get you to sell it!" he said hastily.

Then her smile came back, softened to approval. Almost to love. "I'm glad. You gave me a bit of a scare there, Wilf."

"No, I want to state categorically that I'll never try to talk you into selling again. You're right to keep it. No one would appreciate it as much as you do."

"Why did you take an option on that other farm if it's not suitable?"

"That was Ken's work, I'm afraid. The farm belongs to Anne's uncle, and—"

"That explains it," she said. "I got the idea he was susceptible to Anne."

"Poor Ken's susceptible to most people, I'm afraid. Since he sees Anne so often, she may have more influence than others. But she didn't egg him on to buy her uncle's farm, if that's what you're thinking."

Sage nodded. "Will you look into Helvetia, that farm I mentioned? It has nice rolling hills. I'm not sure it has any sand naturally occurring."

"Yes, I'll have a look. Sand can always be brought in. That's no problem."

"I think I've got all the specimens I want. Shall we have that swim now?" she suggested. "I'm surprised Ken doesn't have a pool."

"Surely you jest! Didn't you see the pool?"

"No. Where is it? I'd love to tour the whole place."

"It's on the other side of the house. I guess the hedge concealed it."

When they returned, Wilf gave her a tour of the house. They passed through stately rooms with Persian carpets on the parquet wood floors and oil paintings on the walls. The music room had a grand piano and a harp. When Wilf tinkled the keys, they discovered the piano was dreadfully out of tune. The whole place, while lavishly furnished and lovely, was slowly sinking into disrepair. The brocade curtains sagged from age, and mildew from the river's moisture was beginning to spot the walls.

"It's like a trip into the past," Sage said, gazing all around. "It's hard to imagine people living like this. Such a shame it's all going to rack and ruin." She shook her head sadly. "You really should develop this property in some way, Wilf."

"I'd like to, but the size is just wrong."

"But there are five acres. It could be expanded, turned into a luxury health spa or something, with additional facilities built on the grounds. Those tennis courts Ken mentioned, for starters."

"The tennis season is short in northern New York. Commercially, it's a doubtful proposition. Maybe the best idea is just to put it up for sale, and let the new owner decide what to do with it."

They changed into their bathing suits and eventually Sage found her way out to the pool. It was an old-fashioned rectangular, concrete pool, finished in Gunite. Empty stone flowerpots at the corners lent it a forlorn air, but it was clean and full of water. There was no heater, and the water was cold. They had only a short swim, and when they had changed back into their clothes, the others were just returning.

Ken looked as if he had got caught in a wind tunnel. His hair was blown to pieces and his cheeks were red. "Lord, I hate boating," he grumbled. "I'm frozen from the wind. Did you find any interesting weeds, Sage?"

She told him about the ginseng. He didn't seem very interested. "I never go into the bush. I tried it once and got caught in poison ivy."

"What time is the company coming?" Anne asked. Sage thought she must have covered her hair with a kerchief. It looked as good as when she had left.

"Nine," Ken replied. "Mrs. Esmond wouldn't cook dinner for so many people, so they're coming later. We'll change and meet on the terrace for cocktails before we eat. I tried to hire a band for tonight, but the only group available was called the Androids. They had shaved heads and wore a lot of chains and things, so it looks like we'll have to make do with records."

Sage didn't think he'd actually hire a live orchestra for a small party. She wore her fancy mint green gown, with her hair piled loosely on top of her head. As she examined herself in the mirror before going downstairs, she wondered what Wilf would think of her outfit. Flower child, he'd called her. She liked that, but she also liked to dress up glamorously once in a while. And Wilf had seemed to like it the last time.

The weekend was going even better than she had hoped. Wilf didn't have any interest whatsoever in buying her farm, so he had invited her here just to get to know her better. It had been a long time since she'd had a serious relationship with a man. What luck that Wilf had spotted her farm from Hooten's helicopter, and come to the Herbarium, and met her. It was all so unlikely, it almost seemed like fate.

Chapter Seven

Wilf wanted to let his colleagues know he had definitely decided not to pursue the purchase of Sage's farm. When there was no answer to his tap at Anne's door, he realized she had already gone downstairs. He went along to Ken's room and heard a grumbling, "Come on in. It's open," when he knocked.

Ken had changed into a white dinner jacket, and was trying to arrange his bow tie. "I see I'm dressed wrong," he said, glancing at Wilf's lightweight summer suit. "Mrs. Esmond had it cleaned special for tonight. She'll be grumpy if I don't wear it. I hate bow ties."

"You look fine," Wilf said unthinkingly. "About Sage's farm, Ken, the deal's off. Completely finished. We're not going to make any offer. She doesn't want to sell."

"We know she doesn't want to sell. That's why she's here, so we can scare her into it."

"No, that's *not* why we're here. It's all been decided. If you get a chance, slip Anne the word."

"What changed your mind?"

"It was a bad idea in the first place. We've never sunk to trying to trick people before. I don't intend to start with Sage. She means a lot to me."

"I see," Ken said, and gave his tie another jerk, pulling one end loose.

"I wish I'd never gone along with this dumb idea of yours."

"Anne's," Ken said hastily. "It was all her idea. I never get an idea. But we agreed there's no harm done. If Sage doesn't want to sell, she doesn't have to."

"She doesn't want to sell, so let's just forget all that and enjoy ourselves."

"Whatever you say." He gave a last tug at his tie and they went downstairs together.

Ken made a beeline for Anne. "The deal's off," he said out of the side of his mouth. "Wilf said to forget it. He's not going to make Sage an offer."

"Why?" Anne asked suspiciously.

"She doesn't want to sell."

"She's just playing hard to get. She's conned Wilf into thinking she likes him, Ken. We can't let her pull the wool over his eyes like this."

"Why would she do that?"

"Innocent lamb," Anne laughed, chucking his chin. "Because men are easy to lead down the garden path when they're infatuated. We have to protect him, or she'll talk him out of a million for those few barren acres she's sitting on."

"Sage isn't like that. She's nice."

Anne looked across the room to Sage. "She's certainly beautiful," she said reluctantly. "But she looks like a siren in that dress. I know a couture gown when I see it. I doubt that innocent babes wear Paris labels, and for sure they don't work for Baxter and Associates. Look at the way Wilf's smiling at her. He's far gone."

"I think he loves her," Ken said, smiling indulgently.

"That could endanger more than his bank account. Do you want him to have his heart broken?"

"Why should Sage break his heart? It's plain as day she's in love with him, too."

"You're a pair of babes in the woods," Anne informed him.

They had their pre-dinner drink on the patio. Anne worked her way to Sage and sat down beside her. "What a lovely dress, Sage. I've been admiring it. Paris, I think?"

"Yes."

"It must have cost the moon. I wish I could afford dresses like that."

"I splurged," Sage admitted.

"Are you enjoying your visit?"

"It's a lovely place," Sage replied, "but I keep thinking what a waste it is, just moldering away here. I suggested to Wilf that he might develop it as a luxury health spa."

Anne nodded. "You're a clever businesswoman. It certainly has potential," she agreed. "It's a shame to waste good land. Wilf says *you* have a bigger spread than you'll ever use. Why not sell him the extra?"

"I plan to cultivate it all, eventually."

"He pays top dollar, you know. Just between us girls, what did he offer you for your place, Sage?"

Sage hesitated a moment, then mentioned the approximate figure.

"What would you actually take?" was Anne's next question.

"I'm not interested in selling."

"We women have to stick together. I won't tell him, dear," Anne said in a confidential tone.

"You can tell him if you want to. He already knows."

"Come on, now," she laughed. "Everyone has their price. You can't be making much, selling herbs."

"I get by," Sage said coolly. She was coming to the conclusion she didn't care much for Anne Fine. When May and Hal appeared, she excused herself and joined them.

Wilf added himself to the little group, and soon pulled Sage away from the others entirely. "Did I happen to mention you look exquisite?" he asked. She was in her sophisticated mode tonight. Not the child of nature, but an alluring, sophisticated woman. He hardly knew which he liked better.

"What, this old thing?" she said facetiously.

"Lady, what you do for that old thing is worth the price of a Super Bowl ticket on the fifty-yard line."

"I'm not so sure of that," she said, feeling both flattered and embarrassed. But she was glad she had chosen to wear the designer original and that it was so greatly received. Wilf's approval was written all over his face. "I hope I'm not overdressed. Is it going to be a large party?"

"I understand fifty are invited. There shouldn't be more than a hundred."

"Surely he won't have gate-crashers so far from the city?"

"No gate-crashing is necessary. Ken urges his guests to bring their friends. He likes crowds." Sage just shook her head. "He has so much, yet he seems very dissatisfied."

"It's hard to be satisfied when you're not doing something useful with your life," Sage said.

"Maybe what he needs is a wife and family to give him a focus." Wilf was surprised when he heard himself say those words. He had spoken instinctively, and that's what had come out of his mouth.

He had always considered his work the focus of his life, but since meeting Sage, he was coming to realize work wasn't enough. This was the first time he had given up on a project he was keenly interested in without a good fight. That should have been his warning. He had put her happiness before his plans, and he felt a deep satisfaction at his decision.

It was only a vague reference to marriage, of course, but Sage was glad to hear that Wilf realized the importance of family. When she looked at him, she had the feeling he was studying her, to catch her reaction. "Yes, a wife and family might do it. It would give him something besides himself to think of," she said, making it a generalized statement. If he wanted to make it more specific, she felt he'd do it later, when they were alone.

Wilf had been worried to see Anne speaking to Sage. Whatever Anne had said, it apparently hadn't bothered Sage, but from curiosity he said, "I saw you talking to Anne Fine. How do you like her?"

"She's all right," Sage said. "A pretty sharp businesswoman, I think."

"And loyal to her friends," Wilf added. He sensed Sage's lack of enthusiasm. Anne was a good friend as well as his secretary. He wanted Sage to like her. Sage just smiled.

Dinner was announced before he could resume this discussion. It was an elaborate meal, even more elaborate than lunch. It began with a rich pâté served with an assortment of fancy wafers. Sage found the pâté too rich, and just nibbled it. For the main dish, Mrs. Esmond had prepared Rock Cornish hens, stuffed with wild rice.

"I feel like Henry the Eighth," Ken said, dismembering a leg.

This led Hal to a dissertation on the British monarch and the dining habits that had led to his ill health.

A white wine was served with the hen, followed by a sweet wine for dessert. Sage was afraid she'd become dizzy, after having had an aperitif before dinner, and refused the dessert wine.

Ken's concern was where to dance after dinner. "Do you think the patio will be a good place, Anne, or inside?"

"Since it's such a nice evening, let's dance outside," Anne said.

"I hate dancing in the wind," he complained. "The wind from the river is cold at night."

"Since you're just having records, why not have dancing both places? Do you have a spare record player?" Sage asked.

"I put stereos in the bedrooms one year, didn't I, Anne?"

"Yes, you did," Anne told him.

"There's a dandy one in mine," May said, "but it has so many knobs I don't know how to turn it on."

"They're all like that nowadays," Ken said, happy to have found a new complaint. "You have to be an engineer to work them. As to VCRs!"

After dinner, the men busied themselves removing the carpet from the living room floor and bringing down a stereo and speakers from a spare bedroom. They set it up on the large veranda, while the women helped rearrange the chairs.

"That man needs a keeper," May said, shaking her head at Ken's extravagance. "Imagine, he didn't even know he had all those stereos. If he weren't so young and slovenly, I'd marry him."

"A waste of time," Anne told her. "I've been... seeing him for years."

Sage just smiled. She wasn't surprised. She already suspected Anne was very interested in money.

"The one who might have some luck in that direction is Sage," Anne said, studying Sage in a calculating way. She noticed that Sage didn't pay the least bit of attention to this idea, as a sharp woman would. "He was left millions, you know," she added enticingly.

After a moment Sage said, to change the subject, "Do you work, Anne, or are you a lady of leisure?"

Now why was Anne looking at her in that strange way? "I do some secretarial work," Anne said. She looked almost embarrassed. "I was a secretary before I married. I don't have any children, so I like to get out of the house."

"I was a schoolteacher," May said, and talked about that for a while.

The stereo was soon blasting out music, and the guests began arriving. It was a very mixed party. There was an eclectic grouping of everything from older men in white dinner jackets and women in party dresses to younger people in shorts and jeans. The crowd soon sorted themselves into two groups. The teenagers took over the veranda, where they danced to rock music, and the others went into the living room.

"Which do you prefer?" Wilf asked Sage.

"The noise level is a little high for me out here," she said. The music was loud enough to drown out the noise of the teenagers.

"Thank goodness. I was afraid I'd betray my advanced years if I suggested we go inside."

"There's not that much difference in our ages!"

"I was hoping you might say you prefer older men."

"I prefer *young* older men," she said, studying him. Older seemed the wrong word. Wilf was fully mature, with an air of authority. "Or maybe I mean older young men."

"I must fit in there somewhere."

He took her hand and they went inside. Echoes from the veranda were still audible, but not loud enough to interfere with the other music. They danced to romantic ballads, oblivious to the milling throng. It seemed to Sage that she and Wilf were in a private cocoon, cut off from the rest of the crowd.

They hardly spoke, but their bodies communicated all the things they were feeling. She was acutely aware of his arms, holding her close. His fingers were warm and possessive on her bare back. When their legs brushed intimately, she felt a thrill shiver through her. They moved in harmony, as if they were one.

Wilf inclined his head and asked softly, "Are you having a good time?"

"Lovely." She sighed, warming to the glow in his eyes.

"I'm glad you came."

"So am I."

"What do you say we take a stroll down to the river?"

"A good idea," she agreed without hesitation, although she knew the river was only a pretext for being alone.

They slipped out the door and around the side of the house through the shadows, down to the river. It gleamed darkly in the moonlight. A cool breeze whispered through the trees, releasing a resinous scent, but it wasn't the wind that caused that frisson up Sage's spine.

"I really shouldn't have brought you here," Wilf said with a rueful smile.

"Why not?"

"It might remind you of our first—no, second—date. The picnic fiasco on the island. You were a good sport about that, Sage."

"I figured your heart was in the right place. You were trying to show me a good time."

"You're half right. I was trying to give you a pleasant evening, but my heart wasn't in the right place. I was just after your property at the time. I guess you think that's a pretty dirty trick to play on a nice woman?"

"Oh, I figured out what you were up to. I admit I was annoyed at the time. I don't like to be taken advantage of."

His determination to confess suffered a setback. He wanted her trust and good opinion, and most of all, he didn't want to lose her. She had never looked lovelier. The more he got to know Sage, the more he admired her. And even if he hadn't admired her character, he still loved her. The realization had dawned slowly. He had never been in love before—not like this. There had been infatuations, of course, but not this hunger, this yearning to protect and cherish someone.

"No one likes to be taken advantage of," he agreed. "I feel very badly about..." He hesitated, afraid he'd shatter the mood, and afraid she might not believe that the whole thing wasn't his idea.

Moonlight gleamed on her pale face, adding an aura of innocence to her beauty. What kind of fool was he, to ever think this woman was a schemer? "I'm sorry for—"

She reached out and took his hand. "No harm done," she said trustingly. "You didn't exactly twist my arm. It's reassuring to see how your conscience bothers you, Wilf. I could never... care for a man who didn't have a conscience."

"Do you think you could come to care for me?"

She looked up into his rugged face, lit with love, and knew she already cared very much. "Yes, I could."

His arms folded around her, drawing her against him. "Don't be angry with me, Sage," he said. His voice, dropped to a hush, was a muffled breath in her ear. The pent-up emotion in it sent shock waves reverberating through her.

She cradled his dark head between her hands and gazed at him in the shadows. "It's all right, Wilf. I understand."

"I really don't want to lose you," he said.

It wasn't a declaration of love, but Sage felt it might as well be. His tone was more than just sincere; it was resonant with determination. A man didn't use that voice, he didn't look at a woman in that manner unless he really cared. A smile moved her lips. "Don't worry, you're not going to," she said just before their lips met, each going halfway in an agonizingly slow pantomime, as if prolonging the moment by mutual agreement.

It was the kind of kiss that she had dreamed of. A powerful, shattering, sincere kiss that stirred her to the vital core of her being, and sent her head reeling. A mellow warmth washed through her as the kiss deepened to passion. There was no self-consciousness, no holding back the surge of emotion that engulfed them. She abandoned herself to the pounding assault of his embrace.

His compelling male warmth held her as if she had been drawn into a magnetic force field. His arms pressed her against him until she was unsure where her body ended and his began. It lasted a long time, yet when he stopped, it hadn't seemed long enough. They just looked at each other with a dazed smile, shocked by the intensity of the passionate explosion they had unleashed. Words seemed superfluous.

"Shall we go back inside?" she asked.

"Sure," he said, and they returned slowly to the dance, stopping in the shadows for another stolen kiss before entering.

Wilf held her more closely when they danced again. Sage closed her eyes to block out all sensation except the exquisite warmth of his two arms around her, his strong chest pressing against her, his shoulder beneath her head, his chin nuzzling her cheek, too engrossed to bother with words. She wished the clocks could stop ticking and they could dance for days.

Sage assumed the party had been a success. When she looked around much later, the room was nearly empty, except for Ken, who was fiddling with the stereo.

"We're having something to eat outdoors," he said. "There's still some chili left. I hated having to disturb you two. You looked tired. I'm pooped myself. It is getting pretty late."

Sage and Wilf exchanged a laughing look. Wilf said, "Thanks, Ken. We'll be right out."

"Better hurry. It's nearly gone," he said, and left.

"I guess it was my closed eyes that made him think I was sleepy," Sage said.

"Do you really want chili?"

She didn't particularly want chili, but mostly she didn't want to be with a noisy group of strangers. She wanted to be alone, and hug her happiness to herself.

"No, I think I'll just go to bed. What time is it?"

"Two o'clock."

"That late! Good heavens, we must have been dancing for hours."

"Hours, minutes. Time stood still for me."

They walked to the staircase, with Wilf's arm around her waist. The chandelier painted prisms on the marble floor below. "Good night, Wilf," she said.

"See you tomorrow. Sleep tight." He placed a light kiss on her forehead, and she went upstairs in a trance.

Once in her room, Sage removed her gown and laid it over a chair, too tired, or distracted, to hang it up. She felt drugged with happiness, and love.

Wilf went out to the veranda, where Anne and Ken accosted him.

"Are you going to marry her?" Ken asked bluntly.

"Yes, if she'll have me."

"Are you sure she's not using you?" Anne asked.

"Don't be ridiculous," was Wilf's answer.

"Well, I got the impression she was all right when I talked to her," Anne said. "She didn't seem to be a calculating type at all. Never blinked an eye when I mentioned Ken being a primo catch."

Wilf looked apologetically at Ken, who smiled, unoffended.

"So we don't mention why we really invited her here," Anne said.

"I'll explain that myself," Wilf said with a stab of concern. He could truthfully say he had invited her because he wanted to be with her, knowing full well that had been part of the original plan. He had also been interested in getting her property. Would he have invited her if he hadn't wanted it? Possibly not—and he would have missed out on love.

"Why bother saying anything?" Anne asked.

"Because if the situation were reversed, she'd tell me. That's the way Sage is, and she'd expect the same of me."

It was the only cloud on the relationship. Wilf dreaded confessing, but he felt confident she'd understand. He wanted to tell her the next morning, but Hal cajoled them all into going to the golf course. He bought them lunch there, and when they got back to Shangri-la, it was time to leave.

May said, "We'd better get packed and go, Sage. You have that shipment for California to see to."

"Yes, we really must go. I had a fantastic time, Ken. Thanks for having us."

"It was my pleasure. I fancy I'll be seeing you again," he added, with a smile at Wilf.

"You just say the word and we'll be here," May assured him. "Be sure you drop in any time you're near Sanville."

They went upstairs to pack, and when they came down, the thanks and farewells were repeated, then Wilf walked Sage to her car. It had been driven around to the front of the house. May remained discreetly behind to leave them alone.

"That went pretty well, all things considered," Ken said to Anne. "I think she—"

May gave him a questioning look. Anne hastily threw herself into the breach, before Ken could say anything revealing, but Ken had been looking at Sage when he'd said "I think she—"

"Yes, Mrs. Esmond handled the extra company in her usual capable fashion," Anne said.

"I guess you've been here before, Anne?" May asked.

"Dozens of times," Ken said. "She practically lives here."

"I've known Ken for ages," Anne explained. "We're old friends." She chattered on about other visits, to keep Ken from talking.

At the car, Wilf put Sage's suitcase in the trunk and opened her door. "I didn't know you drove a Porsche until you arrived," he said. "I was on the lookout for your van."

"This is a holdover from my business days. I left the van for the man who's minding the farm for me."

"When will I see you again?" he asked.

"You know where to find me. I'm usually at home. Are you very busy these days?"

"I'll make a point to get to Sanville very soon, and often. I'll probably be looking into that farm you mentioned. Helvetia. If it's available, I'll soon be working near Sanville," he said.

"That would be nice. We could see each other more often."

"Yes that would be very nice indeed."

He placed a kiss on her cheek. "I'll call you tonight, to make sure you got home safe and sound. Drive carefully."

"I will." Sage was sad that they didn't live closer together. A momentum had been building between them, but with time and space also between them, she was afraid they'd lose something precious. "Did you say you'd be looking at Helvetia soon?" she asked.

As if reading her mind, Wilf said, "Very soon. I'll give it a look when I'm down visiting you. You know my way—a little business creeps in when I'm out enjoying myself."

May joined them and Wilf held open her door, then went around to Sage's side to hold hers. When she got in the car, he reached out and touched her cheek. It was like a caress. He couldn't say more in front of May, but his eyes conveyed the emotion threatening to surface. "Drive carefully," he repeated.

"I will."

She turned the key and waved as the car drove away. In the rearview mirror, she saw Wilf standing, looking after her.

"I hope Ken likes the preserves I took him as a present," May said. "It hardly seems enough after that extravagant weekend, although he was touched at the thought. What can you give a man like that? He has everything—except common sense. He'll end up married to Anne Fine if he doesn't watch himself."

"Wilf says she's all right."

"I got the idea that she's up to something."

"What do you mean?"

"I don't know, exactly. She just gave Ken a squinty look when he started to say something about you. At least, I think he meant you. She jumped in as if to stop him."

"He's pretty outspoken. She was probably just trying to save my feelings, although I don't know why he should be saying anything against me."

"Neither do I. I'm probably imagining things."

Sage's mind was on other things. "Wilf's coming to have a look at Helvetia soon," she said, smiling.

"I wonder why," May said with a knowing look.

They bumped along the twisted lane until they reached the highway. Other than a stop at a roadside stall for strawberries, they reached home without incident. Whiskers was at the gate to meet them. May scooped him up into her arms and took him inside to give him a treat.

Sage was happy to see a good number of cars outside her market store. She admired her knot garden for a moment, and looked happily at the house her grandpa had left her, with the little vine-covered pergola where she had first talked to Wilf. She found Percy before going into the house, and learned he had everything under control. It felt good to be home, back in a house of manageable proportions, even if they did have to do their own cooking.

That evening, they just had toast with eggs cooked up in a herb omelet and served with fresh tomatoes. Since the menu had consisted of meal after meal of rich foods, they enjoyed the simple fare. In the evening, Sage did some research on dill for a future column, while waiting for Wilf's call. It came at eight o'clock.

"Hi," he said. "I guess you made it home all right."

His voice brought a mental image of him sharply before her. "Yes, are you still at Shangri-la?"

"No, I've left, and aged a couple of hundred years, according to Hal. I'm in Buffalo. I wish I were there in Sanville with you."

"So do I."

"I'm tied up with meetings tomorrow. I'll get down as soon as I can. I have something I want to say to you, Sage, but I think it would be better if we could talk in person."

The breath caught in her throat. She was sure he was going to say he loved her. "Couldn't you tell me on the phone? Give me a hint at least?"

Her playful tones told Wilf she had no idea what he meant. "I'd rather be with you," he said.

"All right. I'll be waiting."

"I think something special happened to me this weekend, Sage."

"I think it happened to both of us," she said, and waited. Maybe he would say it after all.

"We'll talk soon. Good night, Sage."

"Good night, Wilf."

Sage wore a dreamy look when she hung up the phone. It occurred to her that if she and Wilf were going to have a relationship, the matter of his living in Buffalo would present a problem. She couldn't move her farm, and he probably wouldn't want to move to Sanville.

But that was something they could iron out when the time came. For now, she was happy to know that the something special that had happened to her this weekend had also happened to Wilf. Love would find a way.

Chapter Eight

Sage felt as if she were living in a golden dream over the next two days. Her farm was expanding and prospering. Percy, who was worth his one hundred and eighty pounds in gold, had found extra employees. She knew from her days in business consulting that as a business expanded, you had to assign authority to others. No one person could do everything. From her back door she could hear the hum of the tractor, tilling those ten extra acres.

Her column was picked up by another newspaper, and best of all, she was becoming more sure by the moment that she had found love. The only thing lacking to bring her dream to life was that Wilf couldn't be with her.

When she met Mrs. Steinem in Sanville that afternoon, she stopped for a chat, hoping to discover whether she and her husband were interested in selling their farm. "How are things at Helvetia?" she asked.

"Not so well since Paul took ill," Mrs. Steinem replied.

"I hadn't heard your husband was ill. I'm sorry to hear it. I hope it's not serious?"

Mrs. Steinem shook her head. "We're not as young as we once were, Sage. The place is too much work for him, and it's so hard to find good help nowadays. We've had to sell off most of the herd."

Sage could feel a quick sympathy with that. "It must be hard to part with them."

"It is, but they've become a rope around our necks. Cattle need constant work. Farming is for youngsters."

Sage could see that the woman was weary, and was happy she could offer some possible relief. "I know someone who might be interested in buying the farm, if you're thinking of selling," she said.

Mrs. Steinem looked interested, but suspicious. "Not one of those developers! Our neighbors wouldn't thank us for landing a high rise on them."

"It would be for recreational use," Sage said vaguely. She remembered Wilf's wish to keep his plan a secret from competitors.

"What price do you think...?"

As Sage wasn't in a position to make an offer, she could only say, "I really don't know that."

"It would have to be enough for us to live on. We'd have to rent an apartment, or buy a condo. I hate to think of leaving the farm. We've lived there ever since we were married. I'll miss my garden, but I know it's time for us to retire."

"I'm sure my friend would offer a good price. He's a very conscientious man," Sage said proudly.

"Your beau, is he?" Mrs. Steinem asked archly.

"I suppose you could say that. If you are interested in selling, Mrs. Steinem, would you give me first refusal?"

"What's that, dear?"

"Would you let me know first, before you sell to anyone?"

"I certainly will, Sage. I'll mention it to Paul. What sort of recreation did you have in mind? Horses, was it? I remember you used to visit that stable near our place when you were younger. You always used to say you'd like to raise horses one day."

"I'd still like to," Sage said vaguely. It seemed rude not to give Mrs. Steinem a clear answer, so she said, "I'm afraid the exact use of the land is a secret, in case of competition, you know. That's why I asked you to let me know first, and give my friend a chance to meet any offer you might receive."

"I understand. I promise I won't sell to anyone else without telling you first. I must run along now and get Paul's prescription filled at the drugstore."

"I hope he's soon feeling better. Tell him I was asking for him."

"I will, and I'll give you a call and let you know what Paul says about selling."

Sage continued on her way home, sorry for the Steinems, but since they would soon have to sell anyway, she was glad she could steer them to an honest buyer. She didn't have to worry that Wilf would take advantage of their situation, as some buyers might.

Wilf had called her again the night before. He had wanted to come to Sanville today, but some business had come up, and he wouldn't be able to come for a few days. He was unhappy with the delay in seeing her, and so was Sage. The glow of loving Wilf hadn't begun to fade, but there was always the worry that time might dim it. He was to phone tonight and to let her know when he could come.

She decided she wouldn't mention Helvetia to him until she heard from the Steinems. No point in raising his hopes if it came to nothing. When he called, they both agreed they hated being apart.

"And tomorrow I have meetings both morning and afternoon. I'll try to get down in the evening. I don't suppose you could fly in and meet me for lunch?" he said, joking, but the wistful tone in his voice told Sage how much he missed her.

"I would if Sanville had an airport," she said.

"Hmm. That sounds like a new project for Jameson and Company."

Phone calls were better than nothing, but hardly enough. She wanted to be with him again. The memory of last weekend was in danger of becoming an obsession.

Mr. Steinem phoned the next morning and expressed a keen interest in selling Helvetia. Of course, his main concern was price, and there Sage couldn't tell him much. She decided she'd drive into Buffalo and meet Wilf for lunch, to give him the news in person, and to get some idea of what price he had in mind. He seemed to be busier than she was, and she was willing to make the effort. It helped that Percy was working out so satisfactorily. In fact, she hoped to hire him full time when he graduated next spring.

The idea of going to Buffalo occurred to her while she was on the phone with Mr. Steinem, and as soon as she hung up, she said, "I'm planning to run into Buffalo and meet Wilf for lunch, May."

May looked up from the table where she was making bran muffins from scratch. As in all her culinary efforts, she had made a colossal mess. The whole table was sprinkled with flour, which was all that kept the spilt milk from reaching the floor. "You'd better call him and make sure he's free," she suggested.

"He said last night he was. I want to surprise him. Would you like to come along?"

"Two's company, three's a crowd."

"You have lots of friends there. You could call one of them downtown," Sage said, because she really wanted to be alone with Wilf. "Wilf's office is right downtown. I have his business card."

"I'll stay home and burn these muffins instead. Hal invited me for a game of golf. Since you'll be away, I'll take him up on it. He doesn't talk so much on the golf course."

"Whatever you like, but you're welcome to come."

Sage felt a flurry of excitement to be preparing for a visit to the city again. She hadn't bought any business outfits since taking over the farm, but her work wardrobe was along classic lines. With a dotted scarf and jade earrings, her taupe linen sheath was still in fashion.

She brushed her long hair up into a smooth chignon and applied her makeup with a light touch. Nylons and high heels felt uncomfortable at first, since she'd become accustomed to cotton socks and sneakers. But the heels made her feel more feminine, and for this special occasion, she wanted to look as feminine as possible.

As she gave herself a last look in the mirror, she thought she wouldn't look too out of place in a fancy restaurant. She felt Wilf would take her someplace special, for this special occasion. More than once she had wished they were together, so he could say what he wanted to say. He had never told her he loved her, but his eyes—his whole behavior—had said it.

It was enjoyable cruising along the highway in her sports car. She was glad she'd kept it, because if she and Wilf were going to have a relationship, she'd probably be making quite a few trips into Buffalo. She wouldn't leave all the commuting up to him, especially when he was so busy.

Too busy, really. She smiled when she realized she was taking such a proprietary interest in him. It wasn't that she would try to change him, even if she had the right. She liked his hard-driving energy. With her experience, she might even be able to help to him occasionally.

Like this Helvetia deal, for instance. He'd be proud of her perspicacity in getting first refusal. Mr. Steinem had promised he wouldn't sell to anyone else without speaking to her first, and he was the sort of man you could trust. If she had Wilf's power of attorney, she could arrange the purchase and save Wilf a trip. She felt a tingle of excitement at the memory of past business successes. She admitted she sometimes missed that wheeling and dealing aspect of her work. Too much of it was harrowing, but just once in a while, it would be fun.

Sage was thankful for her car's maneuverability in the heavier traffic of the city. She arrived just before noon, and had to drive around for five minutes before finding an empty parking space in a lot close to Wilf's office.

She found the office tower without any trouble. It was a soaring slab of glass and concrete, with a directory posted in the marbled lobby. Jameson and Company had one of two penthouse suites, the best suites in the building. He must be doing pretty well. She knew the rent in these places. Her stomach gave a familiar lurch as she rose up in the elevator to the top floor. Her high heels clicked along the tiled corridor to a glass door bearing the company's name.

When she pushed it open, she found herself ankle-deep in a creamy carpet. Oak paneling surrounded the entrance foyer, where the receptionist awaited her. A pert young woman greeted her.

"I'd like to see Mr. Jameson," Sage announced.

"Do you have an appointment? Mr. Jameson is in conference at the moment."

"No, I don't have an appointment. I'll wait."

"His secretary will give you coffee," the receptionist said. "Mrs. Fine's office is to your right."

"Mrs. Fine?"

"His secretary, Mrs. Fine," the woman repeated.

Sage frowned, and waited a moment before proceeding. It was obviously not Anne Fine. She would have mentioned it last weekend if she worked for Wilf. Since she was an old friend of Ken's, Wilf's receptionist was probably some relation. Sage walked on to the office the receptionist had indicated.

At the desk, she saw a familiar crown of sleek coppery hair, and the familiar face of Anne Fine. It seemed odd that Anne was here, but Sage thought she was probably meeting Ken for lunch. There was nothing odd in that, except that Anne gave a lurch of surprise, and stared at Sage as if she were a devil.

"Sage! What are you doing here!" she exclaimed, and jumped up from her desk.

"I was just going to ask you the same thing, Anne." She noticed the letters in Anne's hand and said, "Do you work here?"

"I told you I was a secretary."

"Yes, you mentioned it. Are you filling in for the regular secretary?"

The phone buzzed, and from the way Anne snatched at it, she seemed eager for the respite. "Will you get the Harry Kane file for me, Anne?" a voice said. Not Wilf's voice, but Ken's.

"Right away, Ken," Anne said, and hung up the phone. Her face was bright pink with embarrassment.

The receptionist had called her Mr. Jameson's secretary. She was obviously familiar with the whole operation. So what was the big secret about her working here?

"Sage, I can explain," she said.

"I wish you would. I'm curious."

"There was no harm in that party at Shangri-la. Wilf wasn't trying to buy you out. He just wanted to get you in the right mood so you'd sell him the part of your land you weren't using. He wasn't trying to gyp you! He was ready to pay over market value. You know how these things are done, just courting a client."

Sage felt a humming in her ears. Just courting a client. That's all it had been. That walk with her through the meadows, the dance, the moonlight walk to the river, the long distance phone calls—all "just courting a client." And she had misread it as being a great romance. "I see," she said, in a small, disbelieving voice. At least he'd never told her he loved her.

A door to the right opened, and Ken's balding head peeked out. "Can you get that file, Anne?" he asked impatiently. Then he spotted Sage. "Sage! What the devil are you doing here? Did Wilf talk you into selling after all?''

Anne gave him a quelling look. "I'll tell Wilf you're here, Sage," she said, and turned away.

"Don't bother. I was just leaving," Sage said, then hurriedly escaped into the reception area, with Anne's voice trailing after her. She felt tears spurting, and when she spotted the ladies' room, she went in to recover in private.

She felt as if a mule had kicked her in the stomach. The phrase "courting a client" kept replaying in her head. That's all it had been. Wilf hadn't invited her for that weekend party because he wanted to be with her. He had just wanted to get her farm. And she had thought he was so thoughtful, asking Aunt May to chaperon. It was all a scheme to disarm her.

He had brought his secretary along to feel her out. She remembered Anne's confidential little chat. "What would you really take for the place? Everyone has their price." How could she have been so mistaken about him? All he ever wanted was her farm, and he was willing to do whatever he had to do to get it, including pretending he loved her.

Those tender, solicitous phone calls, wishing he were with her. Obviously the purpose of those confidential talks had been to keep her in a receptive mood until he could change her mind about selling. She felt like a fool for asking Mr. Steinem to give her first refusal on his farm. Wilf never had any intention of buying Helvetia, and she had raised the expectations of a sick, old man for nothing.

In her office, Anne said to Ken, "I'd better let Wilf know she's here."

"He's in conference. He doesn't want to be disturbed."

"He'll want to know this," she said, and went to tap lightly at Wilf's door.

His clients were just leaving. "What is it, Anne?" he asked, mildly curious.

"It's Sage Cramer."

A smile lit his eyes as he reached for the phone. "Put her right through."

"She's here, in person."

An eager grin broke through. "Really? I didn't know she was coming to town. Show her in."

"She's not exactly here, at this moment," Anne said. "She asked for you, but when she saw me—I'm sorry, Wilf. Maybe I should have told her I was your secretary—at Shangri-la, I mean. Ken made some dumb joke about you having talked her into selling her farm and she just bolted out."

Anne had never seen her boss in a rage before. She thought he'd be the kind who turned red and flung his arms about and shouted, but he didn't. He turned as white as a ghost, and seemed frozen to the spot. For a minute he didn't say a word. He just looked as though he was impersonating a ticking bomb. When he finally spoke, he didn't chastise her. He said in a flat voice, "Where is she?"

"The receptionist says she's in the ladies' room. Shall I go after her?"

"No, this is my fault. I'll go myself."

He strode out of his office, down to the receptionist, rehearsing his excuses and regretting he hadn't told Sage the whole truth in the beginning. "Is Miss Cramer still inside?" he asked.

"The blond lady who wanted to see you? Yes, she hasn't come out yet."

"I'll wait," he said, taking a seat. He sat, just staring at one of the big glass windows, with nothing but blue sky beyond, wondering what on earth he could say, or do, to convince Sage he wasn't as bad as circumstances made him look. He should have told her sooner; he *knew* he should have told her at Shangri-la. She would have understood then. She said she understood that he had done more or less the same thing when he took her on that ill-fated picnic.

After three or four minutes of stony silence, the receptionist said, "Shall I see if she's still in there, Mr. Jameson?"

He stared at her in disbelief. "Is it possible she might have left?"

"I had to go to the supplies room to get some pencils."

"Yes, you'd better see if she's still there."

The powder room door opened and the receptionist came in. "Mr. Jameson can see you now," she said, her eyes wide with curiosity. "He's waiting for you at my desk."

"I've changed my mind. I no longer want to see him. You can tell him that. Thank you."

The receptionist looked dissatisfied, but she took the message verbatim. "She no longer wants to see you, Mr. Jameson."

His jaw firmed in determination. "I'll wait. The only way she can get out of there without seeing me is if she flies out the window."

"Shall I tell her?"

"Yes, please."

The door opened again. "Mr. Jameson says he'll wait."

"I don't want to see him," Sage said more emphatically.

"I told him that. He said the only way you can get out without seeing him is if you fly out the window."

Sage didn't answer. She just went to the window, wishing she could fly out. This was ludicrous. How dare he bar the door to keep her in here?

"So what'll I tell him?"

Sage's patience broke, and with fire in her eyes she said, "Don't bother telling him anything. I'll tell him myself."

She pushed the door open and charged into the reception area. Wilf jumped to his feet and went to meet her. "Sage, I want to explain!"

"Your secretary has already explained, Mr. Jameson. I'm not a complete ignoramus where business is concerned. I understand the policy of courting a client very well."

"It wasn't like that!"

"With your secretary disguised as a friend, and your business partner along? Sorry I put you to so much bother. A whole weekend wasted, when you could have been out flattering some other gullible woman."

"But it wasn't like that! I wanted to be with you." She tossed her head in derision. "All right, that may have been a part of it, but once we—"

"Big of you to admit, when I already know!"

"You said yourself courting clients is standard business practise."

"Yes, courting them openly at dinner, when both parties know exactly what's going on. It isn't standard practice to let on you care for someone when you're only trying to put a fast one over on her. That's despicable. Even at Baxter's they never went this far."

"Sage, it wasn't like that!"

"Yes, Wilf, it was exactly like that. I told you the first time we met that I wasn't interested in selling. You've hounded and harassed me for weeks, trying to change my mind, and when nothing else worked, you pretended you loved me. You didn't say it, but that's what you meant with that story about wanting to see me in person."

"No, it isn't. I wanted to tell you this—to confess about last weekend. I've been wanting to tell you ever since it happened."

She just stared, with her heart shriveling inside her. He didn't love her. That wasn't what he wanted to tell her at all. "Then why *didn't* you confess? What was stopping you?"

"I was afraid you—you would reach the very conclusion you've reached. That I was only after your property."

"Afraid I'd wake up and smell the stench of your sort of business dealings, you mean. Well, you were right, but my opinion of you wouldn't be quite as low if you'd told me the truth yourself, instead of letting me find out like this."

"I'm sorry. Can't we go somewhere and talk about this? Have lunch."

"I'm a little particular about who I have lunch with. Go find yourself another dupe, Mr. Jameson."

She jostled her way past him and went out the door, while the receptionist goggled, and Wilf just watched her go. Words didn't have any effect, and he could hardly hold her back by main force.

He just watched her go, wishing he could roll back the clock to last week, even last night. If he'd only told her... Why hadn't he? He'd had a dozen chances. The truth was, he had been afraid something like this would happen. He had just been staving off the inevitable.

"I'll be in my office. I don't want to be disturbed," he told the receptionist. "Hold my calls."

"Yes, Mr. Jameson."

Sage was hardly aware of where she was, or what she was doing. She saw a crowd of people converging on a door, and knew it must be the elevator. She wanted to get out of this place, back home. She joined the crowd and was whisked downstairs. When the elevator reached the mezzanine, she followed the throng out of the building onto the jostling streets, and found her way back to her car.

Her hands were trembling when she tried to start the ignition. She knew she was in no condition to drive, so she just sat there, trying not to think. Her dream had turned into a nightmare. She had known all along it was only a dream, so why should awakening be so painful?

Later, after the first rush of lunch traffic had let up and she had accepted reality, she bought a cup of coffee and took it to her car, because she wanted to be alone. She hated to cry in public.

The hot coffee only heated the emptiness inside her. It didn't fill it. She felt limp, like a deflated balloon. All the joy had gone out of her day, of her life. Eventually she left the garage and began the drive home, past the same scenery, the same factories and warehouses and later, in the countryside, the same farms she had passed just a few hours before. But what had seemed beautiful in the morning gave her no pleasure now.

She was almost glad when it started to rain. It suited her mood to see tears running down her windshield, as if nature was mourning her loss. It was fitting that nature should weep for nature girl. She had taken the name for a compliment, but what Wilf probably meant was that she was a hick, who was easily conned.

It hadn't rained at Sanville. As she neared home, the roads were dry, and before she reached her farm, the sun had peeped out again. At home, she had to face May, who knew at a glance that something was terribly wrong.

"Wilf was too busy to see you!" May said. "I told you to call before you went."

"He wasn't busy. I saw him," Sage said, and slumped disconsolately onto a kitchen chair to recount the story in a disjointed fashion.

May shook her head in distress. "I can hardly believe it of Wilf. Mind you, I suspected something was afoot with that Fine woman. Didn't I mention it to you, the squinty way she looked at Ken just before we left? She was trying to hush him up."

"Yes, you mentioned it. I should have known myself it was too good to be true."

"I'm so sorry, Sage. But are you sure that's the *only* reason Wilf asked you for that weekend? He really seemed taken with you."

"That was certainly the main reason. He admitted it."

"He was offering a fair price at least. I mean, it's not as though he was trying to gyp you."

"He was trying to pull a fast one, all right. And I fell for it. I should have known better," she said, disgusted with herself.

"It'll be uncomfortable having him around when he offers for Helvetia." May poured Sage a cup of coffee and passed her a burned bran muffin. Sage accepted them without even looking. She took a bite of the muffin without tasting.

"I didn't tell him about Helvetia, and I have no intention of telling him." She looked at the muffin in her hand, wondering where it had come from. "He was never really interested in Helvetia, May. He just pretended he was to lull my suspicions."

"Pity. The Steinems could use the money, with Paul sick and all. Maybe now that Wilf knows you're not going to sell, he might really buy Helvetia."

"That's up to him. I'll phone the Steinems and tell them not to turn down any offers on my account. If Wilf wants it, I'm sure he'll get it. He'll stop at nothing to get what he wants."

May tsked and poured herself a mug of coffee. "And he seemed so nice. I thought you'd really found someone at last. Ah, well, there are lots more fish in the sea than ever came out of it." She passed Sage the cream. Sage picked up her cup and took a sip of black coffee.

"How'd the golf game go?" Sage asked. She didn't want to talk about Wilf anymore. It was too painful. Whiskers hopped up into her lap and she began stroking his fur. Its soft warmth was comforting in her present mood. Maybe she should get a cat of her own.

"About like you'd expect," May said. "My score was exactly double Hal's. He says I should take lessons to add length to my drives."

"Will you do it?"

"I might. Are you interested in lessons at all?"

"No, not really." She doubted she'd ever see a golf course again without remembering this awful experience. "I'm going to change and go outside. I want to walk the meadows, and decide where to do my new planting. With the California contract, I'll have another ten acres under cultivation."

When she went up to her room, Sage shucked off her nylons and high heels with distaste, glad to be free of them. They felt soiled from her recent experience. A cotton T-shirt and jeans were what she was comfortable in now. Leave the city to the sharks. She had found calmer waters.

It was always a pleasure to walk through the fields, planning her future crops. Sweet clover grew up to her knees, and released its heady scent as she walked. Where the tractor had been at work, the rich black earth was freshly turned, waiting for seeds. The lowering sun warmed her head and shoulders. Overhead, birds soared.

A tall row of poplars whispered in the wind, their leaves changing to silver as the breeze revealed their underside. They had once been the boundary between Grandpa and his neighbor. They were so pretty that Grandma had wanted them left intact, even though they made mowing the hay difficult and served no useful function. Sage had no plans to disturb them, either. Beauty was important, and some herbs liked the shade anyway.

By next year at this time, these fields would be full of aromatic herbs that would add to her profit. She'd buy herself a horse, for such jaunts as this. A hundred and fifty acres was a long walk, and she'd want to keep a close eye on her new crops.

Maybe her herbs and her writing and taking long rides astride her horse would be enough to satisfy her. That and adding a cat, or maybe a dog to the house hold would complete the blissful picture she was imagining for herself. Not everyone was cut out for marriage. With time, her farm might grow into a mini empire. She'd be the herb queen of America, and use her marketing skills to manage her business. She gave an ironic smile as she realized that would put her back on the fast track she'd been so eager to escape.

Perhaps then she'd forget this awful ache in her heart. Perhaps.

Chapter Nine

Wilf sat alone in his office, regretting the chaos his life had fallen into. He had finally met the perfect woman. He had even managed somehow to catch her interest, and if he didn't do something, he was going to lose her forever.

He was never one to sit futilely repining for long. When something was wrong, his instinct was to handle the situation, to get busy and do whatever had to be done to make it right. That was how he managed his business life, and it had worked successfully there, so why shouldn't it apply to personal relationships, as well?

Since Sage didn't believe words, he had to show her by his actions that he meant it when he told her he wasn't after her farm. And the best way to do that was to acquire another property for the golf course project. That would prove beyond argument that his only interest in her now was a personal interest. The next step in his planning was to decide what property to buy.

She'd mentioned Helvetia might be for sale. He'd toured that property with Hooten in his helicopter. It was his second choice, if he couldn't get Sage's place. Clever of her to have spotted it. She had a good eye and a sharp mind. He had always preferred intelligent women.

Helvetia had good terrain, and was the proper size. While it would serve a slightly different area, it had good potential from neighboring Rochester. He'd run down to Helvetia tomorrow morning, make his offer, and when the deal was settled, he'd tell Sage. She could hardly refute the evidence if he had it in black and white to show her.

He spent a restless night, often going to the phone and even picking it up to call Sage, but something stayed his hand. Better wait awhile. She needed time to simmer down, to think about the whole situation. Perhaps the memory of that magical weekend at Shangri-la would soften her first bout of anger. She had just learned the facts when she exploded at him, so he had suffered the first heat of her wrath. Waiting was the hardest thing of all for Wilf, when every instinct urged him to action. But this was too important to rush. He had to do it right this time, because it was his last chance.

He phoned to let Anne know he wouldn't be at the office, and set out early in the morning for Helvetia. He passed through Sanville, but his route didn't take him past the Herbarium. He stopped a moment at the side route leading to it, wanting to turn the car down that road, but he steeled himself to stick to his original plan. Maybe by this evening he could go to her with evidence of his innocence. This happy thought lightened the latter part of his trip.

He observed as he entered the gate to Helvetia that it was a prosperous farm. The red brick house was large and elegant, with a fanlight door and big wraparound veranda. The fences were in good repair. That was the sign of a prosperous operation. He couldn't see many head of cattle, but assumed they were pasturing in some other area. The house wasn't set up right for a clubhouse, but it might make a residence for the manager. A perk like that would help them get a good man for the job. It would even make a good country place for himself....

A country place? Since when did he want a country place, away from the hurly-burly of his work? Since he had met Sage Cramer, that's when. He had been envisioning quiet weekends with her, away from the world. Until now, his work had been his life, but he was gradually coming to realize that there were other things worth having. In future, he felt his work would become a means to an end, not an end in itself.

He'd never meant for it to monopolize his whole life. When he was poor, he had wanted to make money, and somewhere along the way, he had let money become an end in itself. He had always thought of himself as a pretty clever fellow. How had he missed seeing such an obvious thing?

An elderly woman answered the door on his second knock. She wore her white hair in a topknot and looked at him with curious blue eyes.

"Can I help you?"

"I'm Wilfred Jameson," he said, handing her his card. When she had read it, he added, "I'm looking for some land hereabouts to develop for recreational purposes. I was wondering if you'd given any thought to selling Helvetia. It's a handsome farm."

"Thank you. As a matter of fact, Paul—that's my husband—has decided to sell. Won't you come in, Mr. Jameson?"

Wilf was introduced to an elderly man who showed the ravages of ill health. Mrs. Steinem served coffee, and Wilf repeated his business.

Mr. Steinem thumbed the card. "What price did you have in mind, Mr. Jameson?"

"I've looked into the price that farms in the area are going for. Of course, I realize yours is a finer spread than most." He mentioned a generous offer.

Mr. Steinem looked not only satisfied, but delighted. "That's about what I had in mind." He smiled. "I'll get back to you. I've promised another customer I'd let her know before making a deal."

Wilf felt a flutter of anxiety. Now who the devil was onto his plan?

"Miss Cramer is a neighbor. We've known her family forever, and we can't go back on our promise," Mrs. Steinem explained.

"Miss Cramer?" Wilf asked, jerking to attention. Doubts and confusion whirled through his brain. What did Sage want with Helvetia?

"Yes, she's interested in raising horses, I believe. I was talking to her the other day and she asked me to give her what she called first refusal."

"I see." With great effort, he managed a smile. Never let them see you sweat. "Then you'll be letting her know of my offer?"

"We certainly will, Mr. Jameson. More coffee?"

"No, thank you. It was very nice meeting you both."

He took his leave, frowning in consternation. As he had stayed at the Belview when he was in Sanville before, he returned there for lunch. Not that he was hungry, but he wanted time and quiet to think over this newest development.

Sage had tried to arrange to buy Helvetia? When had she done it? "The other day," Mrs. Steinem had said. Sage hadn't mentioned this last weekend. She must have done it very recently. Maybe as recently as yesterday afternoon, when she'd returned from Buffalo...

She had done it to spite him. What other reason could there possibly be? She had never mentioned raising horses. With her herb business expanding, that would take all her time and money. There would be a good deal of money required to develop the extra land required to fill that California order.

This was just a childish revenge because she was angry with him. But it was poorly arranged. He would have thought Sage was intelligent enough to get an option. First refusal meant virtually nothing. Oh, it might boost Steinem's price a little, but not enough to prevent Wilf from outbidding her if he really wanted to. Unless she had a partner... Who did she know with that kind of money? The name Mike Baxter soon occurred to him.

Wilf ordered a steak and ale, but he didn't eat much. He just pushed the meat around on his plate and nibbled a little of the accompanying salad. He figured the Steinems would have contacted Sage by now. They seemed pretty eager to sell. What would she do? He wanted to see her, to confront her face-to-face and tell her what he thought of her.

At the farm, Sage put off the unpleasant phone call to the Steinems for as long as she could. By noon hour, her conscience nagged her into phoning and explaining.

"That's all right, Sage," Mrs. Steinem said cheerfully. "I was just going to call you. I would have done it sooner but Mrs. Armstrong dropped in and we got to discussing the fall fair. I had a tentative offer this very day, so don't feel badly."

"Oh, I am glad!" Sage exclaimed. But beneath her pleasure, she also felt a wince of regret. Now there was no hope of Wilf buying it. He wouldn't be spending any time near Sanville. Some recalcitrant corner of her heart had nourished a hope that proximity might yet bring them together.

"We don't know much about the deal yet," Mrs. Steinem said. "I'll let you know as soon as it's settled. I have to give Paul his lunch now."

"Say hello to Mr. Steinem for me."

"I will, dear. Thanks for calling."

Sage hung up and said to May, "It turned out all right, after all. The Steinems have had another offer."

"I'm glad to hear it. Who's buying it?"

"Oh, I didn't think to ask her," Sage said. Her mind had been on other things. "Mrs. Steinem was in a bit of a hurry," she explained.

"Lunch is ready. I made sandwiches and opened a can of soup."

"That's fine," Sage said, and exerted herself to normal conversation as she ate.

Sage tried to push the whole matter out of her mind, and take some consolation from the Steinems' good luck. But work was always the best way to lose her problems, and as soon as lunch was over, she returned to her office. She laid a large sheet of paper out on her desk to make a map of her land, marking the type of soil and the amount of sun each plot received.

She poured over her books, marking down exactly the requirements of the herbs she planned to plant. The elder liked a sunny, moist location, so it wouldn't do in the shade of the poplars. The elder and sorrel could grow side by side in the sun. For the shade, the lemon balm would do fine. It would get enough morning sun to keep it from becoming blanched. She'd talk to Percy about planting, whether to propagate, buy rooted plants, or just plant seeds.

She was just putting her books aside to go and look for Percy when she heard the tap at her office door and May peered in. "Company, Sage," she said in a strangely excited voice.

Glancing over May's shoulder, Sage saw Wilf staring at her with somber, dark eyes. She tamped down her anger. How dare he come here? He had a lot of gall. She stared back, momentarily bereft of speech. She had to work to keep her anger at full pitch, because at the first sight of him, her whole body told her to rush into his arms.

As she watched him silently, she noticed the strange expression he wore. She hadn't expected him to come at all, but since he had come, she thought he would at least have the grace to look sheepish or apologetic. The face that confronted her might have been set in concrete. It was rock hard, and defiantly angry. If it weren't for the shadow of doubt in his eyes, she would have said he had come here to argue. Did he actually think he could browbeat her into selling, after all that had happened between them?

"I don't believe I have anything to say to Mr. Jameson," Sage said coolly.

Her speech was enough to dissipate the last of his self-control. If she thought she was going to get away with this unscathed, she didn't know her antagonist very well. "I have something to say to you," he declared and strode boldly past May into the office.

May discreetly closed the door and shamelessly hung about outside to overhear what was said.

Wilf stood, arms akimbo, and glared at Sage. "That was a pretty low trick, Sage, and not as well executed as I'd expect from one of Mike Baxter's protégées."

"I don't know what you're talking about. I'm not one of Mike Baxter's protégées!"

"Oh really? I figured you'd probably called in your old boss as your partner. I didn't think you could afford to set up a stable on your own."

Sage just stared at him, bewildered. Had he lost his mind? "Did May tell you I was thinking of buying a horse?" she asked in confusion.

"A horse?" He laughed grimly. "You'd hardly have to buy two hundred and fifty acres to stable one horse."

"Hardly, since I already have several acres of my own, and a barn, as well."

"Then you were acting solely on Mike's behalf?"

"I left Baxter's two years ago. I haven't seen hide nor hair of Mike since then. What is this all about?" She knew by Wilf's sneer that he didn't believe her. If she hadn't been so curious, she would have been even angrier than she was.

"You dropped the ball, Sage," he announced triumphantly. "Next time you plan to snap up a property from the competition, you should take an option on it. First refusal isn't worth the air it's written on."

"First refusal? Are you talking about Helvetia?"

"What else? Have you papered the whole countryside, getting first refusal on all potential golf courses in the area to spite me?"

"So that's it," she said quietly. "You've been to see the Steinems. And you think I'm as underhanded as you are. I don't deal in that sort of skulduggery, Wilf. I leave that up to your sort. I have absolutely no interest whatsoever in what you do, as long as it doesn't involve me."

"Then why did you—"

She didn't want to admit she'd been so keen to help him, but as she had to give some reason, she told him the simple truth. "I did it for you, since you said you were interested. I wasn't in the position to take out an option, although I realize that would have tied the property up securely. I phoned Mrs. Steinem at noon today and told her to forget the whole thing. She told me she'd had another offer, but since I had no interest in it, I didn't ask for a name."

"For *me?*" he asked. He hadn't even heard the rest of her explanation. She said she had done it for him, and he believed her. That explained everything.

"Before I realized it was really my place you wanted all along," she said with a glare.

"But I didn't! I explained that. I told you what happened."

"You didn't tell me anything I didn't already know," she pointed out. "You only confessed after I found out what you were up to. Now that I know how you operate, I'll advise the Steinems to get themselves a good lawyer."

Again he regretted his mismanagement of his dealings with Sage. Now he had a new offense to explain, as well. "What was I supposed to think when the Steinems told me you had first refusal?"

"What any normal person would think. That I was trying to help you. I'd mentioned Helvetia to you last weekend. You said you were interested. When Mrs. Steinem told me her husband was ill, and she was interested in selling, I tried to secure it for you. It's called friendship, Wilf. You should try it sometime. There's more than one way to do business."

He was overwhelmed with regret. Buying Helvetia was supposed to bring them together, but it had only driven them farther apart. "Sage, I'm sorry." His hands went out in a futile gesture of apology.

She looked at him and shook her head sadly. "You're always sorry, Wilf. There's something very wrong with the way you operate when you're always having to apologize for what you've done."

"But I had no idea—"

"I know," she said, fighting back a tear. "That's the part that really hurts. You had no idea that I'd try to help you, when we were...were friends," she said, stumbling over the last word. "The first—the only thing—that occurred to you was that I was stabbing you in the back. I don't think this relationship is going anywhere. You don't trust me, and after what's happened, I certainly can't trust you."

He wanted to apologize again, but swallowed the words "I'm sorry." That would only make things worse. "It was all a misunderstanding," he said.

"Yes, it was. I thought you liked me."

"I loved you, Sage. I still love you. I thought, at Shangri-la, that you felt the same way."

Her first flush of joy at his words soon faded. This man didn't even know the meaning of the word love. "And you still thought I was scheming behind your back with Mike to sabotage your plans?" she asked, incredulous. "What kind of love is that?"

"I know you don't want to hear it, but I really am sorry, Sage. It's just that—" He shook his head ruefully. "Maybe I've been in this business too long. We were potential business associates before we were friends. No business associate has ever gone out of his way to help me before. I guess I was looking for the angle."

"So it seems. There's no angle. Go and buy Helvetia, if that's what you want, but just don't try any fast stunts on the Steinems."

"I'm not a crook!"

"I know you haven't broken any laws. I wasn't planning to call the cops. Goodbye, Wilf."

She turned away and picked up a book, to show him the meeting was over. Wilf stood a moment, looking at her, wondering if he should try again to explain. But he sensed that any further explanations would soon become an argument, so he reluctantly turned and left. His heart felt heavy with regret.

Really there was no explanation to make. Everything Sage had said was true. He had invited her to Shangri-la partly for the purpose of courting a client. Of course, he hadn't loved her then, or at least he didn't know he loved her. He thought she'd realize why he'd invited her. When had things changed? Was it when she got out of the car and kissed him on the cheek? He hadn't expected that. It seemed to put the visit on a different footing.

Or had it happened when they were walking through the meadows, and she had looked so wistful when she thought he was going to try to persuade her to sell? No, by then he had already decided he loved her, and didn't want her to even suspect the visit had any other purpose than seeing her. That was when he had begun feeling guilty.

One thing he was sure of was that he hadn't tried to use love as a lever for business. How could she even think such a thing of him? It was just her frustration and anger twisting her thoughts. The same thing had happened to him.

The first thought that occurred to him when the Steinems told him that Sage had first refusal was that she was trying to outwit him. As if she wasn't experienced enough to take an option, if that was what she had in mind. He had insulted her intelligence, as well as her integrity.

There *was* something wrong with the way he acted when he had to constantly apologize for his actions. Some mistrust of humanity had crept into his life, and this was the result. He didn't even recognize honesty and goodwill when he met them. He actually thought Sage, who wouldn't pick the endangered ginseng, had gone behind his back to sabotage his business.

He had accused her of being Mike Baxter's cohort, when she had explained why she'd left Baxter's in the first place. He hadn't trusted the woman he loved. That's what it amounted to. As she so rightly pointed out, what kind of love was that? Not Sage's kind. She deserved better.

May had scampered back to the kitchen when she heard Wilf coming to the office door. She went to meet him as he left. "Would you like a coffee before you go, Wilf?" she asked. Her eyes were bright with interest.

"I think I'd feel better if I get out of here, fast. Thanks anyway, May."

"We'll take it outside where we won't be disturbed," she said with a meaningful look.

"I don't think—"

"She won't leave her office," May said, making her meaning perfectly clear. Then she darted into the kitchen and poured two cups of dark, heavy coffee. She looked assessingly at the burned bran muffins and decided against them.

They sat in the shade of the pergola, where Wilf had had his first meeting with Sage. He noticed the sun shining through the leaves, making them semitransparent. He hadn't noticed before how pretty they were. Sage had awakened him to the beauty of nature and the lovely bucolic scene surrounding them. A warm breeze riffled the vines as they sat side by side in a pair of wicker chairs. Filtered dots of sunlight danced on the dewy lawn below.

"I really made a botch of it, May," he said, lifting his eyes to gaze into the distance. "The only woman I ever really loved, and I managed to turn her off."

A smile flickered over May's face at his words. "She's pretty upset all right. Where'd you get the crazy idea she was setting up a stable?"

How did she know that? "I guess we were speaking pretty loudly," he said.

"No, I was eavesdropping," she admitted shamelessly. "It's true she wants a horse. Sage mentioned Mrs. Steinem thought she was going to open a stable, since Sage likes to ride, and she couldn't explain, since you wanted your golf course kept a secret. She told me what happened in Buffalo. Too bad you hadn't told her sooner. Those sorts of shenanigans always come out, sooner or later. I suspected long ago, when Anne quizzed her about what she'd take for the farm."

Wilf frowned. "I hope Sage doesn't think I put Anne up to that!"

"Odd you never mentioned Anne was your secretary."

Wilf blinked in surprise. "I thought you knew! It was no secret. Surely it must have come up sometime over the weekend."

"No one mentioned it. I even asked Anne what she did. She said she did some secretarial work. She didn't mention where."

"The fact is," Wilf said, "Anne thought Sage was trying for a higher price. I dare say Anne was trying to protect me, but I didn't ask her to do it. Sage didn't mention she'd worked for Baxter. When Anne discovered that—"

"Sage didn't stay long once young Mike took over."

"I know. She explained that to me later." He turned to face May. "Do you think there's any chance for me, or should I just bow out gracefully?"

"I tried to whitewash you as best I could, but she wouldn't hear it."

"Why did you bother trying?" he asked, mildly curious. He sipped the coffee, hardly noticing how awful it tasted.

"Because I like you. You may not be lily-white, but you're no worse than most. The main reason, though, is that it's plain as the nose on your face that she loves you."

His first quick flush of hope soon dimmed to doubt. "I sure didn't get that impression," he said.

"You don't know her as well as I do. And you didn't see her when she got back from Buffalo that day. She looked as if she'd been beaten with clubs, Wilf. She's been dragging herself around, trying to keep herself interested in her herbs, but it's a trial for her. I can tell. She tries to act tough, but she isn't really. Put some more sugar in that coffee if it's too bitter for you," she said, passing the bowl.

"It's fine," he said, and took a small sip to appease her.

"Sage has been hurt a lot in the past, Wilf. Her father and mother got divorced when she was quite young. She had a rootless life until she came here and lived with her grandparents. You were trying to buy the only security she's ever known when you tried to buy the farm, although you had no way of knowing that, of course. Maybe she didn't know it herself."

"She must think I'm heartless. She never told me all that. She did mention that she'd grown up in a commune. I got the impression she'd enjoyed it. I know you mean well, but I think you just convinced me it's hopeless."

"I didn't take you for a quitter," May said challengingly.

Wilf studied this quaint little woman, and felt she was trying to goad him into something. He also felt she wanted to befriend him, and he didn't plan to lose another friend if he could help it. May knew Sage intimately. If anyone could help him, she was the one.

"What can I do to win her, May?"

"What do you do when you're having trouble in a business deal?"

He considered it a moment. "Raise the price, throw in a few perks, whatever it takes. But this isn't a business deal."

"Still, is there any reason you couldn't throw in a few perks?"

"How can I? That would only make things worse. I'm definitely not trying to buy her farm now."

"I didn't mean *that*," May said impatiently. "The perk I had in mind was marriage. You know, as proof of your good faith and intentions."

He looked nonplussed. "She'd throw a book at my head."

"A book won't kill you. How is she ever going to know how you feel if you don't tell her? If you just walk away from it, she'll think she was right. That you were only after her property. Maybe that's all you were after," she goaded, her tone making it a question.

Wilf just looked his reproach. "I can't propose to her in her present mood."

"Oh no, not right away. I'll need to have a while to soften her up. Give the Steinems a good price, even though they are desperate to sell. That'll show her your heart's in the right place."

"I planned to give them a good price," he said, offended.

"Relax. I'm on your side, Wilf. And on her side, too. I'll make her see sense. Do you have to go back to Buffalo right away?"

"I'm willing to stay as long as it takes."

"Good. Then I'll call you at your hotel. If you're out buying Helvetia, I'll leave a message. I don't imagine you'll be just idly sitting by the phone with doughnuts. A busy, intelligent man like you."

Wilf cast a suspicious glance at her, but he saw only approving admiration. "I'd planned to make an offer—a generous offer—for Helvetia while I'm here," he said.

"Hal will be glad to hear he's going to get a decent golf course." Her smile suggested a personal interest in Hal.

"Are you and Hal—"

"He asked me to marry him. I agreed, if he'll promise not to bore me with his lectures. I've had enough of the schoolroom. My interest in fostering this match between you and Sage isn't completely altruistic. I hate to go off and leave her alone. I haven't even told her he's offered. She's too upset. I'd like to think she has someone to take my place. Oh, I don't mean in the kitchen. A shaved ape could cook better than I can. She just needs someone to be there for her."

"You have an applicant for the job, but whether she'll have me..."

"We'll be in touch. You'd better run along now. I'm burning a pot roast today. I'd like to ask you for dinner, but that would be rushing it."

"I'll be waiting by the phone—with doughnuts. Thanks a million, May."

"I'll expect to be matron of honor at your wedding."

"You've got a deal." They shook hands. Then on an impulse, Wilf reached down and kissed her cheek before leaving.

May's offer of help cheered him somewhat, but he was afraid it was mere wishful thinking on her part. Sage wasn't the sort of woman who'd sit back and have her husband chosen for her. Especially a husband she didn't trust.

Chapter Ten

May tried to discuss Wilf's visit over dinner, but Sage didn't feel up to it. It took all her self-control to eat. Every bite lodged in her throat. When compliments on the pot roast didn't stop May's questions, Sage adroitly detoured the conversation to work instead.

"I want to sound Percy out about coming to work for me when he graduates," she said. "I wonder what salary he'll expect. I doubt if I can match what the big nurseries and government are offering, with agriculturalists in such demand. I'll point out that herbs are a growth area. It'll be good specialized experience for him."

"Maybe if you threw in the van for his personal use after work he'd take a little less," May suggested.

"That's a good idea. He mentioned he likes the atmosphere here at the Herbarium. You know, the sort of family feeling. We should invite him and his girlfriend to dinner some night, May."

"Court the client, you mean?" May asked with a sly look. "Sure, why not? It's standard business practice, I believe. You'd better do the cooking."

A flush of annoyance bloomed on Sage's cheeks. She wasn't sure May had overheard her argument with Wilf, but she was familiar with her aunt's snoopy ways, and suspected. "Yes, there's no harm in it," she agreed, "as long as it's done quite openly."

"Not quite openly," May pointed out. "Your real intention in asking Percy to dinner is to suggest we're all one big happy family. You don't plan to adopt him, just hire him."

"He's twenty-one, a little old for me to adopt," Sage said.

"True, but you *are* getting on, Sage."

"I'm only twenty-four."

"Twenty-five next month. A quarter of a century. Seems old for a bride to me. Of course, girls married younger in my day. But then, I guess you've settled for your work, expanding your crops and all."

Sage eagerly snatched at this straw. "It's very rewarding. In any case, I'm much too busy to think about marriage right at the moment."

"That's how I felt when I started my great career of teaching. I was too busy working up from teacher to department head to think of marriage. I've often regretted it. It's lonesome, when you get to a certain age and are still coming home to an empty house. Then you decide to get a cat for company. First thing you know, you're too old to have children. Oh, by the way, if you want a kitten, the Newtons' cat has had a litter."

"I certainly plan to have children! I love kids."

Sage looked so sad that May was almost sorry for that last gibe, but it was for the girl's own good. "Really?" she asked, her eyebrows lifting. "Then you won't want to wait much longer to get your family started."

"The pot roast is good," Sage said, to change the subject. "What herbs did you use?"

Sage had a nose for herbs. That she had to ask told May that her mind was on other things. "I tried putting in some rosemary, as you suggested."

May dropped one last hint about marriage after dinner. When they were clearing the table, she said, "I'm playing bridge at Hal's place tonight. Don't wait up for me. You don't mind, spending so many evenings alone, I hope? You have your work, and Whiskers will be around if you want company."

"I'll be busy," Sage said. But there was an edge of wistfulness in her voice.

She felt forlorn when she went to her office. Whiskers was nowhere to be seen. Some company! It was depressing, being alone in a big house in the country. Sometimes she regretted having left the city. Not often, but sometimes she just wanted to get all dressed up and go out on the town.

She didn't feel like doing any research or writing that night, so she went out onto the veranda and sat alone, listening to the crickets and watching the fireflies in the bushes, and thinking of Wilf.

Courting a client wasn't so terrible. Maybe he hadn't been trying to trick her. There hadn't been anything special between them before that weekend. She had certainly been interested in him, probably more interested in him than he was in her, or she would have realized why he'd invited her to Shangri-la. If she hadn't liked him so much, she would have realized it. It was her partiality that colored the invitation in a different hue.

Wilf hadn't even kissed her when she arrived. She was the one who'd made the first move. She couldn't really gauge his reaction behind those sunglasses. He was probably shocked to death.

And once he had begun to fall in love with her, he hadn't put any pressure on her at all to sell. No one had actually lied to her. Wilf hadn't mentioned that Anne Fine worked for him, but as she recalled their conversations, she remembered that nothing remotely connected to that had come up when she was with Wilf. Their conversations had been more personal. It might have been an oversight. It was Ken who had actually introduced her. "This is my friend, Anne Fine," he had said. And added something about her being a special friend. The conclusion both she and May had reached was that Anne was just a friend, but that didn't prevent her from also being Wilf's secretary.

Sage could forgive the events of Shangri-la, but how had Wilf thought she was trying to beat him out on Helvetia? She'd never do a thing like that to a friend. She'd outmaneuvered a few business associates in the past, of course. Everyone did that. It was called being good at your job. Alert, a go-getter, clever.

She had hardly acted like a friend when they'd parted in Buffalo, so why would he expect her to act like one? She hadn't mentioned Helvetia to him at all when she was there. It must have come as quite a shock to Wilf when Mrs. Steinem told him of her interest. The last thing he'd think was that she was trying to help him. Wilf knew she'd worked for Baxter, of course. That might be where he got that idea she'd double-crossed him.

Sage decided she wasn't much of a friend herself. A friend would have stayed and listened to his reasons in

Buffalo. She wouldn't have stormed out of the office like a crazed woman.

She had half forgiven Wilf, but not enough to call him. Calling him was tantamount to an apology. He was probably back in Buffalo by now anyway. And she was here, alone, worrying about May's not-so-subtle little hints. She was slowly but surely growing old. Her biological clock was ticking off the years. She didn't want to make her work her whole life. She didn't want to end up with a cat or a dog for company. She wanted a husband. Dammit, she wanted Wilf Jameson, warts and all.

She wanted her own work, too, but she wanted very much to be a part of Wilf's busy, exciting life. She still got a charge of adrenaline when he talked about his business deals. She had always been attracted to those strong, forceful men. Maybe because her own father was so unsatisfactory in that respect. She wouldn't want the whole onus of being in charge of massive developments when she was raising a family, but she would like to be a part of it.

At eleven, she decided to go inside and brew a pot of chamomile tea to help her relax. She planned to be in bed before May returned to pester her with more sly digs about losing Wilf. She called Whiskers, and scooped him up into her arms to take indoors. Even Whiskers seemed to reject her that night. He hopped out of her arms as soon as she opened the door, and fled to his favorite chair in the living room to wait alone for May's return.

At the Belview, Wilf sat by the phone, not with doughnuts, but with a headache. He wished he had some of that soothing tea Sage had served him once. Chamomile tea, she'd called it. He remembered the peace and serenity he had felt on her patio the night she'd invited him to dinner. The landscape was a patchwork quilt of various shades of green, with such a sweet-smelling breeze coming from them.

He had never shown a bit of interest in her work. She must think he was the most self-absorbed creature she'd ever met. The only plant he could remember was ginseng, the one she wouldn't pick. That and the chamomile tea. It would be nice to come home to a place like Sage's garden after work. Nicer to come home to a woman like Sage.

He settled for a Scotch and water, but it didn't help him sleep. Neither did his relaxation exercises. After two tries, he decided to try to remember the names of the wildflowers Sage had shown him. The yellow one had a French name, and five leaves. A white one had a little speck of blackish red at the center, to deceive the insects.

In the morning, Sage was in the kitchen when May came down. May noticed immediately that she looked as if she hadn't slept a wink.

"How did the bridge go last night?" Sage asked dutifully, but her mind was obviously elsewhere. Those dark smudges under Sage's eyes told the story.

"Not great. I got stuck with Ralph Henson for a partner. He doesn't know a spade from a club. He kept calling the club a shamrock. He trumped every trick I played. My own partner."

"That's too bad."

"What did you do last night, Sage?"

"I just relaxed. It was so nice out."

"I thought maybe Wilf would have given you a call," May said, peering at her niece from the corner of her eyes.

Sage tried to look disinterested. "No, he's probably gone back to Buffalo by now."

"Don't you think he'll stick around and finalize the offer on Helvetia while he's here?"

Sage looked interested. "Maybe he will," she said. But the glow soon faded from her eyes. "Mrs. Steinem said she'd let me know. She hasn't called. He'll probably want to take it to his lawyers for advice."

"Not necessarily. Wilf must know the ropes himself. Mrs. Steinem would only call you after Wilf has left," May said, and poured herself a cup of coffee. She was glad Sage had made it. Hers was always potable. She was also happy to see that Sage was in a mopey mood. Sage was disappointed with the way things had turned out, and that meant she still loved Wilf.

"I think you were a little hard on Wilf," May said, with a tentative peek to see whether her niece was ready to discuss it.

"I guess maybe I was," Sage agreed wanly. "It was sneaky of him not to tell us Anne was his secretary though," she added, as if to justify her position.

"I believe that was Anne's own idea, Sage. I always thought there was something fishy going on with Anne and Ken." She wanted to say more, but didn't like to reveal that she'd been talking to Wilf. "I think it's generous of Wilf to look after his cousin. Ken must be a wicked trial to him," she said, to throw Wilf into a good light.

"Yes," Sage agreed, but she looked as if her mind was a mile away.

When she went outside, May phoned the Belview. "Wilf, it's me."

"How is it going?" Wilf asked eagerly.

She knew from his tone it wasn't an idle question. "She's softening. The only objection she raised today was that it was sneaky of you not to tell her Anne was your secretary. I couldn't explain or she'd know we're in cahoots."

"I've been thinking about what you said, May. If she thought I was purposely concealing my business connection with Anne, it does make me look pretty sneaky."

"Somebody was sure concealing it."

There was a silence from the other end of the phone while Wilf pondered the situation. "I seem to remember we discussed it earlier. Didn't we talk about Anne always trying to sell me her uncle's farm?"

"Something was said about it, but what's that go to do with Anne working for you?"

"I don't know. Nothing, I guess. I just assumed Sage knew. No wonder she was so angry when she saw Anne in my office. She must have thought the whole weekend was a setup. It wasn't like that." He gave a rueful tsk. "Well, maybe it was something like that. I *was* hoping she'd reconsider when I invited her."

"I understand. Are you going to settle the deal for Steinem's place today?"

"I'm on my way there now. I was hoping you'd call."

"I'll call again later. Maybe tonight's the night. Percy helped."

"Who? Who's Percy?" he asked.

"A man she's planning to hire. I've got to go now. Hang tight, Wilf."

"If I were any tighter, I'd snap."

It was just before dinner that Mrs. Steinem called Sage.

"He bought the farm!" she exclaimed, gurgling with delight.

"Oh, I am happy for you, Mrs. Steinem. I hope you got your price."

"More than we expected. And you'll never guess what, Sage. Mr. Jameson—that's the buyer—is letting us have the use of the house for as long as we want. Isn't that grand? We won't have to move. Oh, he explained there'll be a bit of commotion with the golf course being prepared, but that'll suit us just fine. It'll be an interest for Paul. A bit of excitement for him. Something to watch when his cows are all gone. He's such a nice man, that Mr. Jameson."

"Is the deal all signed and everything?" Sage asked, hoping to learn if Wilf had left the neighborhood.

"We just signed on the dotted line. You're the first one I called, since I told you I would. I'm going to call my sister now. She'll be glad to hear we're not moving, since she lives just down the road."

"Thanks for calling," Sage said, and hung up the phone.

That was really thoughtful and generous of Wilf to have given the Steinems the use of the house. She liked to think she was a caring person, but that idea hadn't even occurred to her when Mrs. Steinem mentioned disliking having to move.

She told May the news.

"Isn't that nice," May said. "Just like Wilf, to let them use the house. I always thought he had a kind streak in him. I remember how he helped me look for Whiskers, and rescued him from the pear tree. A man who likes animals makes a good father."

"Yes, he'd make a good father. The deal is closed, so he's probably gone back to Buffalo," Sage said. Her eyes wore a sad, faraway look.

"Or he might still be at the Belview," May said blandly. When Sage looked interested, she waited a few minutes before saying, "What do you say we drive into Sanville tonight to see the bright lights? All two dozen of them."

"I have to type my column," Sage said. "You go ahead. Take my car if you like. I let Percy use the van."

"Maybe I'll do that. I need some cream rinse for my hair. The bleach is hard on it. I'll pick up something to read while I'm there. Do you need anything?"

What Sage needed couldn't be picked up at the corner store. "No, thanks. I'll clean the kitchen tonight, May. You might as well go while it's still light out."

May repaired her makeup and left. She drove directly to the Belview and asked for Wilf. He came to the lobby to see her, excitement shining in his eyes.

"I bought the Steinems' place—on generous terms," he announced.

"I know all about it. That was nice of you, Wilf, to let them use the house."

"How did you know?"

"Mrs. Steinem phoned Sage. She was impressed. She's alone at the house, and she can't leave, because she lent Percy the van, and I've got her car."

"Who is this Percy?" he asked, his brow furrowing in concern.

"Nobody you have to worry about. I can't keep myself busy for long in this hick town, so you'd better get out to the farm right away. I think I've got her softened up for you."

"I just left. Thanks, May."

"Don't forget, I'm to be your matron of honor."

"And I'll be your best man, if you like."

"You've got a deal, but I'm not interested in a double wedding. I don't want any other bride taking the shine out of my day. I've waited too long for it."

May smiled contentedly as Wilf dashed out the door. In a triumphant mood, she went into the bar and ordered a glass of wine, which she drank all by herself. Let the other customers think what they liked. She was no longer a schoolteacher. A professor's wife could have a glass of wine in a public place if she wanted to.

With another long evening alone to get in, Sage took her time clearing the table and stacking the dishwasher. She cleaned the sink and wiped the counters, and thought about mopping the kitchen floor. May was such a haphazard cook that it was usually littered, but tonight it only needed sweeping. These routine jobs helped her concentrate when she was considering an important problem.

What she had to decide tonight was whether she should call Wilf, since it seemed he wasn't going to call her. It would be foolish to let pride stand in the way of their future happiness. If she could only be sure he'd welcome the call, she'd pick up the phone that very minute. What stopped her was the fear that he'd be coolly distant. She didn't think she could take that.

She thoughtlessly lifted her hand and wiped her brow. Until she felt the perspiration, she hadn't realized how hot it was in the kitchen. She opened the window, then decided to go out on the patio and catch the evening breeze.

* * *

When Wilf called, no one answered the door. Since May had assured him Sage would be home, he assumed she hadn't heard him knock. Maybe she was in the kitchen. He went around to the rear. As he turned the corner, he saw her on the patio, just gazing quietly into the distance while a breeze riffled her hair. She looked forlorn and vulnerable. He wanted to rush forward and hold her in his arms, to comfort her.

She wore her hair out long and loose, as she had when he'd first met her. In her jeans and shirt, she might have been taken for a teenager. He remembered her troubled past, and felt a fierce need to protect her. His heart lurched in his chest to think of losing her. He quickened his pace. When he reached the paved path, she heard his footsteps and turned to see who was coming.

Wilf stopped and just looked at her uncertainly, trying to read by her expression whether he was welcome. Her eyes widened in surprise, and he waited to see whether the surprise turned to anger or pleasure. When her lips opened in a tremulous smile and she lifted her arms in a welcoming gesture, he ran the last steps to her, took the stairs two at a time, and rushed straight into her waiting arms.

For Sage, there was no doubt. Wilf's eager face told her what she wanted to know. If that wasn't love glowing in his eyes, then she was blind. When his arms closed around her, she felt as if she had found a safe home at last. She clung to him, without either of them saying a word. For a long moment they just held each other tight with their eyes closed, gently rocking, relishing their unique good fortune.

At last she lifted her face to him and he kissed her, while the evening breeze bathed them in the fragrance of her garden. Beneath the heady excitement, Sage felt a deeper sensation of peace such as she had not known since first coming to her grandfather's farm. Now she knew what the essence of that peace was. It had nothing to do with a place, or a job or financial security. It was loving and being loved.

It felt good and right being with Wilf. She had found where she belonged, and never wanted to leave it. The bruisingly tender kiss pressing her lips wasn't the kiss of someone who wanted to take advantage of her, but the giving embrace of a man who loved her. His strong arms and firm chest shielded her from life's vicissitudes.

Sage nestled her head in the crook of his neck and encircled his waist tightly, claiming him for her own. 'I'm so glad you came, Wilf,'' she whispered.

"Darling, I'm going to say it one last time. I'm sorry."

She looked an apology at him. "So am I sorry, Wilf. I've been thinking about things since yesterday. I was angry with you for not trusting me, but I didn't trust you, either, or I wouldn't have stormed out of your office. I would have listened to you. I should at least have listened to my own heart."

"I really thought you knew Anne was my secretary. I realize now how it must have looked to you."

"I thought you were just courting a client. I've done the same."

"A very special client. You. I had an ulterior motive all along. I was really courting the woman I loved. My past experience—and what I knew of yours—signaled to me that you wanted to sell and were only holding out for a higher offer, but my heart didn't believe it. If you remember, it didn't take much to convince me. Just a shoot of ginseng."

"Ginseng?" she asked in confusion.

"When you wouldn't pick it, I knew you were no schemer. I felt about two inches high." His lips nibbled at her ear.

"It didn't take much to convince me you were all right either," she said. "Just a few digs from May—and my own common sense."

"And to think, we nearly talked ourselves out of... this," he said, and placed a kiss on her forehead.

Sage raised her arms and looped them around his neck. Her head lifted and his lips slid down her cheek to touch hers with a disarming tenderness that revealed the depth of his feelings.

"Mmm. That's very nice, Wilf, but I'm not a child," she said enticingly.

"I noticed," he murmured, and crushed her mercilessly against him. His hands slid down to encircle her small waist, gathering her close to him. The kiss deepened to desire. A cardinal warbled to his mate in the gathering twilight. The sound of cars driving in and out of the shop parking lot was faintly audible, and the echo of the phone's buzz came through the door. They didn't hear any of it.

With his arm around her, Wilf led her to the love seat and drew her down beside him.

"I trust you're planning to make an honest man of me, Sage." She frowned. "Bad beginning. What I'm trying to say is that I love you very much. I want marry you." He realized that nothing else had ever occurred to her.

"That'd be nice, I'd like that. I'd also like to have a family... with you." She looked at him for signs of his feelings. They had never discussed having children.

As soon as he had assimilated the novelty of the idea, he smiled. Then his smile stretched to a grin of delight. "I'd like that. Me, a father! We have a few logistical problems to work out, such as where we'll live. With phones and faxes, et cetera, I can work out of your place. I assume you'll want to stay here to oversee your business."

"Yes, but I'm hiring an agricultural student who can take over when I want to be in Buffalo."

"It might be convenient to keep my city apartment for when I have to be in town."

"I'd like to spend a little time there, too—with you, I mean. I wonder what May—"

"She'll be marrying Hal."

"What!"

"Yeah, he's asked her."

"She didn't tell me that! When did she tell you?"

"I must confess, I've been seeing other women behind your back, Sage."

"So May's been pestering you, too, has she?"

"I wouldn't use the word pestering. Keeping my hopes up is more like it. I've also been seeing another lady."

"Mrs. Steinem?"

"You read me like a book."

"That was thoughtful of you, letting her keep the use of the house."

"I was hoping you'd approve." He took her fingers and squeezed them. "Of course, that's not the only reason I did it. A move would have been hard on them, both physically and emotionally. I was in a mood to sympathize with emotional stress."

"You don't have to explain your acts of kindness to me, Wilf. I know the real you. You're just an old softie." She laughed.

"Not that old, I hope! Remember, you're going to make me a father."

"I think you're just the right age for a father—and a husband."

Wilf lifted her hand and kissed her fingers. He had never thought loving someone would feel this way—so deeply peaceful, so right. He had always thought of marriage in terms of being "caught," but it wasn't like that at all. It felt more like winning a lottery.

He felt as if he had won a rare prize, and was humbled that Sage would have him. "At least I'm mature enough to realize I don't deserve you, darling. Did I tell you I love you very much?"

"Yes, you told me by actions as well as words."

"And I intend to go on showing you by my actions. I'll be the best husband a woman ever had."

"I'll hold you to that," she said, shaking a wifely finger at him.

"Just so you hold me real tight."

She pulled him closer to her on the love seat. "How's that?"

"It's fine for starters. This is better."

He gathered her in his arms as the sun sank behind the trees, bathing them in gold dust.

They didn't hear May when she arrived, and when she discovered them on the patio, she thought it best not to disturb them. She'd just slip in and brew a pot of herbal tea for later.

Whiskers darted from the shrubbery to greet her. She gathered him into her arms and slipped quietly into the house.

* * * * *

**HE'S MORE THAN
A MAN, HE'S
ONE OF OUR**

Fabulous Fathers

ONE MAN'S VOW
Diana Whitney

Single father Judd Tanner had his hands full with a houseful of boys and one orphaned goddaughter. But a woman's touch was the last thing he wanted. Women, he knew, were experts at one thing—leaving. It didn't matter to Judd that from the moment she'd arrived, Leslie Leighton McVay had his boys behaving and his godchild smiling. It would take more than that to convince him that the pretty drifter was really home to stay....

Find out just what it takes for Judd to love again, in Diana Whitney's ONE MAN'S VOW, available in June.

Fall in love with our **Fabulous Fathers**—and join the Silhouette Romance family!

Silhouette
ROMANCE™

Take 4 bestselling love stories FREE

Plus get a FREE surprise gift!

Special Limited-time Offer

Mail to Harlequin Reader Service®
3010 Walden Avenue
P.O. Box 1867
Buffalo, N.Y. 14269-1867

YES! Please send me 4 free Silhouette Romance® novels and my free surprise gift. Then send me 6 brand-new novels every month, which I will receive months before they appear in bookstores. Bill me at the low price of $1.99* each plus 25¢ delivery and applicable sales tax, if any.* I understand that accepting the books and gift places me under no obligation ever to buy any books. I can always return a shipment and cancel at any time. Even if I never buy another book from Silhouette, the 4 free books and the surprise gift are mine to keep forever.

215 BPA AJCL

Name	(PLEASE PRINT)	
Address	Apt. No.	
City	State	Zip

This offer is limited to one order per household and not valid to present Silhouette Romance® subscribers.
*Terms and prices are subject to change without notice. Sales tax applicable in N.Y.

USROM-93 ©1990 Harlequin Enterprises Limited

WHERE WERE YOU WHEN THE LIGHTS WENT OUT?

SILHOUETTE SUMMER Sizzlers '93

This summer, Silhouette turns up the heat when a midsummer blackout leaves the entire Eastern seaboard in the dark. Who could ask for a more romantic atmosphere? And who can deliver it better than:

**LINDA HOWARD
CAROLE BUCK
SUZANNE CAREY**

Look for it this June at your favorite retail outlet.

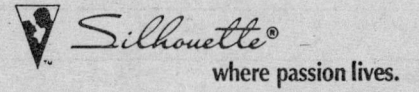

Silhouette®

where passion lives.

Is your father a Fabulous Father?

Fabulous Fathers

Then enter him in Silhouette Romance's

"FATHER OF THE YEAR" Contest
and you can both win some great prizes! Look for contest details in the FABULOUS FATHER titles available in June, July and August...

ONE MAN'S VOW by Diana Whitney
Available in **June**

ACCIDENTAL DAD by Anne Peters
Available in **July**

INSTANT FATHER by Lucy Gordon
Available in **August**

Only from

Silhouette
ROMANCE™

SRFD

A romantic collection that will touch your heart....

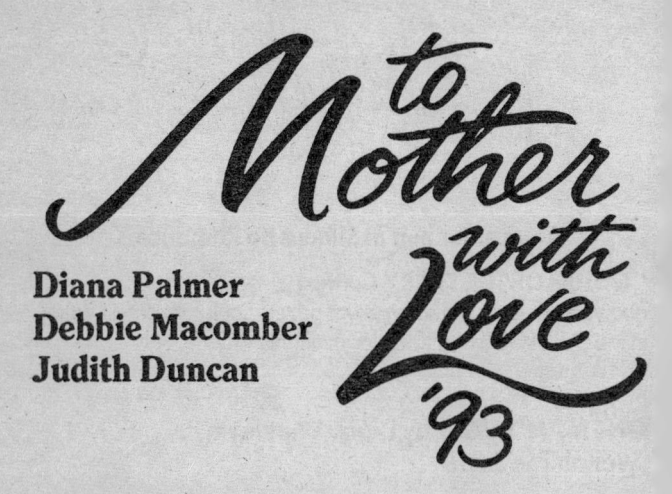

Mother to with Love '93

Diana Palmer
Debbie Macomber
Judith Duncan

As part of your annual tribute to motherhood, join three of Silhouette's best-loved authors as they celebrate the joy of one of our most precious gifts—mothers.

Available in May at your favorite retail outlet.

Only from Silhouette®

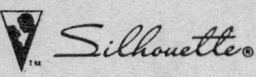

—where passion lives